FORCING YOU YOU AWAY

ARCHER & EVERLEIGH, #1

USA TODAY BESTSELLING AUTHOR
KENNEDY FOX

LAWTON RIDGE DUET SERIES READING ORDER

TYLER & GEMMA DUET

A best friend's brother,
second chance romance

Keeping You Away

Needing You Close

NOAH & KATIE DUET

A best friend's brother,
friends to lovers romance

Pushing You Away

Holding You Close

ARCHER & EVERLEIGH DUET

A brother's best friend,
roommates to lovers romance

Forcing You Away

Wanting You Close

Each duet can standalone, but suggested to
read in order for the best
reading experience.

Wish I'd had met you sooner
So I could've loved you longer
Wish I'd had spent it on you
Instead of wastin' all that time

"Coulda Loved You Longer"
-Adam Doleac

PROLOGUE
ARCHER

FIVE YEARS AGO

As I wait in my car for Annie, I know something's wrong.

My sister was supposed to meet me for lunch twenty minutes ago, and she's not answering my calls. She's six months pregnant and sometimes gets caught up with morning sickness. However, she usually texts me if that's slowing her down. I would've preferred to pick her up, but her drug dealer boyfriend doesn't like me coming around. He knows I won't take his bullshit, so we have to sneak behind Chad's back.

Probably for the best because while I've had this talk with her dozens of times, I'll give her my entire savings today if she'll finally leave his ass. Selling drugs is bad enough, but he also treats my sister like a punching bag. I've seen bruises on her and nearly lost my shit. Right now, I have enough cash to move her away from here as long as she's willing.

After another ten minutes of waiting and five calls sent to voicemail, I hightail it out of the parking lot and drive to her house. The neighborhood's trashed on a good day, but it's all

1

she can afford. We didn't grow up with much, and both got into some trouble trying to survive. However, after high school, Annie got her CNA license and turned her life around. I'll always love and be proud of her, but we fight because of her god-awful taste in men. Perhaps she gets it from our mother. Lord knows Mom couldn't have a stable relationship to save her life. Chad always has an excuse for why he can't pay half the bills, so Annie constantly works overtime at the nursing home to cover them.

I park in front of her place and notice the screen door has been ripped off the hinges. My heart pounds as I race up the porch stairs and see tables and chairs flipped over.

"Annie!" I call out, and when I go into the kitchen, I freeze at the blood pooled around Chad's skull. "*Annie…*"

"Archer, stay there," she orders with panic in her tone.

"Are you hurt?" I ask, eyeing the handgun in her grip. "Give me that."

"I-I didn't mean to shoot him…" Her voice trembles as her hand shakes.

"Annie, gimme the gun," I repeat as calmly as I can.

"He came home and started breaking everything. I'm not sure what set him off this time. It was like he was…"

"High off his ass," I finish for her.

"He grabbed my arm and squeezed me so hard. I cried and begged him to let me go," she explains between sobs. "That only pissed him off more, and he threw me to the ground, then started kicking and hitting me. When I saw the gun in his hand, I thought he was going to kill me."

When she finally blinks up at me, I notice her nose and face are covered in blood.

"I managed to kick him in the groin, and when he fell to the ground, I grabbed it from him."

2

"Annie, it's okay…Give it to—"

"He stood and laughed, but it was a terrifying sound. Said I was gonna pay for that. Threatened to kill the baby. Called me a bunch of names, and when he came for me, I panicked and pulled the trigger."

Tears fall down her red-stained cheeks.

"I shot him in the leg first. He barely flinched, so then I aimed for his head."

"Good. You did the right thing," I assure her. "He would've taken your life, Annie. You realize that, right?"

She stares off and nods, the shock of reality hitting her.

"Annie, it's okay." I hold out my palm, pleading for her to comply.

She slowly gives it to me, and I immediately wipe off her prints with a dish towel.

"Wash your hands," I demand. "I shot him, got it?"

"What? Archer, no." She scrambles for the gun, but I lift it out of her reach. "You'll go to prison. It was self-defense. He was…"

"Kicking your ass," I grind out. "He kicked you in the stomach again?"

She nods, then turns around and lifts her shirt where his shoe prints are embedded into her pale skin.

"The ribs," I spit out. At least he had some decency not to kick the baby.

"And if we can't prove self-defense, you'll be giving birth in a jail cell. Even if you don't get prison time, the strain of going to court could put the baby in distress. Not risking that." I turn her around to face me. "I'll tell them I walked in on him hitting you, grabbed the gun, then shot him twice. With your injuries, it's believable. You need to go to the ER and get an ultrasound."

She covers her belly with her hands. "I can feel her kicking."

I blow out a breath and kiss her forehead. "Thank God for that."

"Archer, I can't let you take the blame."

"You never reported his abuse, Annie. There's no documentation. You shooting him won't be justified without witnesses or a paper trail of repeated behavior. You might get away with claiming self-defense, but without any medical evidence of priors, you could still get jail time. Again, I'm not risking that. You and the baby deserve better. I have twenty thousand in cash. Do *not* use it to bail me out, got it? You take it and get the hell out of here. Away from his family and this town."

"Where did you get that kind of money?" she asks as I put my fingerprints on the gun.

"Don't worry about it, okay? It's yours. Use it." Then I direct her to grab it from my car and hide it before the police confiscate it.

"Archer, I can't do this. What if they don't believe you?" Her face is red and blotchy, and covered in more tears.

"They will. A tatted-up guy from the wrong side of the tracks will be plenty convincing. Chad was beating you, you're my pregnant sister, and that's plenty of motive. As long as you stick to the story, Annie. Understand?" I wipe her cheeks, and she winces at the touch. "Trust me, okay? I need you to do exactly what I say."

"I trust you." She nods. "I just wish you wouldn't do this."

"I'd do anything for you." I rest my palm over her baby bump. "Take care of my niece."

After Annie repeated the story to me without hesitation, I called 911. I told dispatch what I'd done to protect my sister.

Ten minutes later, five squad cars arrive, and the officers get out with their weapons pointing at me. As soon as I walked out of the house, I tossed the gun on the ground and held up my hands in surrender. They charged forward, pulling my wrists into cuffs while reading me my Miranda rights. I don't have extra money for a lawyer, so I'll wait until they can get me a court-appointed one before I talk.

Annie's escorted outside with tears streaming down her face as I'm put in the back of a cop car.

"I love you," I mouth.

"Love you too," she says.

It takes two hours before I'm assigned an attorney. Before the detective questions me, I go over the events that led me to shooting Chad.

"He was uncontrollable and wouldn't stop beating Annie, so I shot him in the leg. When he continued to punch Annie's face, I aimed higher." Since they took my sister to the hospital and can see her bruises, it's obvious that part is true.

"Nevada self-defense law states that you must use no more physical force than necessary to defend yourself or someone else," he informs me. "If it's determined the act is reasonable, then it's legal."

I blow out a breath. "And if it's not?"

"Then you'll be charged accordingly," he states. "You'd have the burden to claim that you acted out of fear for your sister's life, and then the prosecution would have to prove beyond a reasonable doubt that the justification didn't match the threat. Since he was unarmed, shooting him twice could ruin the viability of a self-defense claim."

After being interrogated for an hour, my stomach turns at how they try to trip me up to change my answers. They ask if I had it out for him before he abused my sister, and if it was

5

planned. There's zero remorse, and considering the way they look down at me, I'm not surprised. I have no priors and nothing more than a speeding ticket on my record, yet they're treating me like a serial killer.

"Given the circumstances with your sister, they're offering you a plea deal," the detective returns and informs us. "One that'll avoid going to trial."

My lawyer nods at him to continue as I try to steady my breathing.

"Voluntary manslaughter. One to ten years in state prison."

Manslaughter. Prison. My vision blurs, but I try to remember why I did this.

My lawyer leans in and whispers, "A category B felony means the killing was in the heat of passion and not premeditated. Much shorter sentence."

I nod with understanding because I can't seem to find my words.

"The judge will ultimately decide how many years you'll get, but this plea bargain is your best bet. You'll have court in three days, but until then, you'll stay in the county jail."

Those three nights were terrible, but life was about to get a lot worse.

The judge gave me eight years with the possibility of parole after five.

I'd do it all over again to protect Annie. No amount of prison time would've convinced me to tell the truth about what really happened. Knowing she and my niece were safe is what kept me sane behind those bars. They're all who mattered in the end.

CHAPTER ONE

ARCHER

PRESENT DAY

MY PALMS ARE SWEATY, and I keep wiping them on my jeans as I wait for the plane to deboard. It's been half a decade since I took a flight, and it was just as uneventful as before. I don't know why I'm so nervous, considering Tyler has always been a close friend, but moving to the small town he grew up in is a big deal.

Tyler and I were cellmates, and we kept in touch even after he was released. He's like a brother to me, and we'd do anything for one another. It's one of the reasons I considered moving here, plus I wanted to get the hell away from Nevada. After he offered me a job at the gym he just opened and helped me find a place to live in his hometown, I couldn't say no. It was a chance for me to learn to live again without my past hanging over me like a black cloud.

Eventually, it's my turn, so I grab my carry-on. It's all I brought with me. Though my sister packed all my things into boxes for when I got out, I decided to leave them behind.

Once I'm off the plane, I quickly walk through the airport. I keep my head down, not wanting to draw attention to myself —something I've perfected over the years. Eventually, I find Tyler waiting for me outside. When I'm close, he gives me a tight hug.

"Damn, you're fit as fuck," I tell him with a laugh when he lets me go.

"The benefits of owning a gym, I suppose. Need some help with that?"

"Nah," I say and throw my suitcase into the back seat.

"We'll be in Lawton Ridge in a few hours. How was the flight?" he asks as we buckle, then turns onto the highway.

"It was boring. Slept most of the time. But tell me about you. How's dad life and the new business?" I have nothing interesting to talk about and often prefer to listen, but Tyler already knows that.

He chuckles. "It's amazing. I love being a dad and a husband. It's two of my greatest accomplishments. The gym is growing, and we even have people driving from the next town over to join. Swear everyone in town has a membership at this point, which is a dream come true. Proof that it's possible to start over and find happiness. It's gonna happen for you too, Archer."

I give him a pointed look.

"I'm serious. You've got a job. A place to live. If I can start over, you can too. I wholeheartedly believe that."

"Glad you haven't lost your faith in me."

"You're damn right."

"About the only one who hasn't," I mumble.

"That's not true."

Tyler chats about the weather, and I'm happy for the subject change.

"Ya hungry?" he asks.

"Nah, I already ate. Grabbed a burger before my flight. Can't remember eating something so good after choking down slop for the past five years."

"That's too damn bad. Belinda—she owns the deli and is the one dating Gemma's dad—made her famous shepherd's pie today."

"Oh yeah, I remember you mentioning her before. Does she make it often?"

"All the time when the weather starts changing. It's Southern comfort food at its finest."

"If you say so." I laugh because his Southern accent is starting to come out more now that he's been home. "But I could make room," I tell him, patting my full stomach.

Tyler catches me up with more details of the gym and how great it is being married to the woman he's been in love with for eternity—Gemma. Their baby girl, Scarlett, was born two months ago, and Tyler's already excited to have more kids. I smile, noticing how truly happy he is. Seeing him like this gives me an inkling of hope that maybe one day I'll have the same.

"I was thinking I could pick you up tomorrow mornin' for a tour of the gym. Is six too early?"

My eyes go wide. "That's prison time."

He chuckles. "Or military hours."

Tyler served in the Army for a term after he graduated high school. I think it's why he's so disciplined. Or that could be because he basically raised his sister when he was a kid himself. Something I can relate to as well.

"I'm just kiddin'. Six is perfectly fine. Not like I have anything going on. I think my schedule is pretty clear from now until eternity."

"Great. That's what a boss likes to hear. Oh, did I mention that you'll be staying at my sister's place?"

My eyes go wide because as long as I've known Tyler, he's been overly protective of her. It's why I've always given him shit about it when we'd write back and forth. "At Everleigh's?"

"Yes. And don't get any ideas. She's still off-limits. It's for *your* sake, not *hers*."

It makes me snort. "Should I be scared or worried that I'll be living with your sister?"

"When it comes to Everleigh, *both*. She can be a terror. I really did search for other options, but since it's such a small town, rentals are few and far between. When something became available, they were taken by the time I called. It's like Hunger Games for property in Lawton Ridge. Maybe rentals should be my next business venture?"

"I guess it could be profitable, not sure. And I don't care where I live. At this point, I'd sleep on the street if I had to."

Tyler shakes his head. "I'd never let that happen. I'd give you my couch first. Might struggle to sleep through a baby crying, but earplugs are a godsend," he muses as if he's tried them a time or two.

"Thanks. Appreciate that, man. Honestly, anything's better than a jail cell."

"You're right about that. I remember the first night I was home and how it felt to sleep in my bed. It took a while for me to finally relax, but eventually, I slept like I hadn't since before I was behind bars." He lifts his brow at me. "I was serious about Everleigh, though. No touching. No flirting. And, under no circumstances whatsoever, absolutely no hooking up. It'll only complicate your living situation, trust me."

"You sound like you're chaperoning a high school prom with that stern dad voice."

He chuckles. "It's important that you get your life back together. Everleigh's a distraction and doesn't respect personal boundaries. Believe me when I say she can be a bit much."

"A bit?"

"*A lot*," he corrects. "I lived with her when I was getting back on my feet, and she's very, very particular about things. Overly flirty with anyone who has a penis… Oh wait, never mind, that's not true. She's flirty with *everyone* regardless if it's appropriate or not. I think she has the entire male population wrapped around her finger. It's one of her many flaws."

Now, I'm laughing. "She sounds friendly. Some would call that a personality trait."

"It's not. Everyone basically falls in love with her because of it. It's made my life as her older brother hard as hell."

"So she finds trouble, or does trouble find her?"

"She's her own worst enemy. And needs to stay single for a little while herself. It's actually best for you both."

I hold up my hands. "Okay. Understood, boss!"

After he takes the exit off the highway, we turn onto a narrow two-lane road with a skinny shoulder. Trees surround us for twenty more minutes until it eventually opens up to reveal a small town that looks like it dropped straight out of a movie. Buildings with small shops line the street. There's a deli, supermarket, and a bank. As we pass some people on the sidewalk, they wave at Tyler.

"So, I take it this is an 'everybody knows everybody' type of place?" I glance over at him.

"Oh yeah. Don't worry. They're gonna try to get to know you too. As soon as it gets around that there's a new guy in town, they're gonna be on you like white on rice. The old

11

women at the grocery store are going to hound you with questions like you're on the stand."

"So, watch what I say around them." It's not a question but more of a statement.

"Yeah, they tend to have a way of gettin' information outta you like ya wouldn't believe, but only tell them what you're comfortable with. My close friends have been told about you and are aware of your past, but don't worry, none of them will judge you. Noah did time too and started fresh once he returned. Everleigh has called it the ex-con club." He chuckles.

"Yeah, I remember Noah and hearing about him being locked up too. And thanks for the heads-up. Though I'm sure if people really wanted to find out, all they'd have to do is a Google search." I shrug but remain hopeful. It'd be nice to keep my past where it belongs and not be forced to talk about it.

Once we get to Lawton Ridge, Tyler slows in front of a small shop with an ungodly amount of harvest decorations out front. Several bales of hay are stacked with pumpkins in all different sizes. A giant sign out front encourages people to stop and take photos with the hashtag EVER AFTER.

"That's the place Everleigh owns," he proudly says.

"Looks nice. My sister would love it."

"Yeah, I bet she would. Everleigh's killing it these days and even has plans to expand. Don't be surprised if she tries to hire you."

This makes me chuckle as we turn down another street.

"Does she always decorate like that?"

"Oh yeah. Just wait until Christmas throws up all over her shop. She's always loved the holidays." Soon, he's pulling into a driveway and turns off the engine.

My eyes widen. "This is Everleigh's place?" We're parked

in front of a very nice side-by-side condo on a street with perfectly manicured lawns that screams small-town Alabama.

He nods. "Yes, sir. This is it."

I follow him to the door and notice her porch is just as decorated as her shop. Tyler knocks and turns to me while we wait for her to answer. "Yesterday was her birthday."

"Yeah? Maybe she's not home yet?"

"She's here." Tyler checks the time and grows impatient. Punctuality should be his middle name. Another few moments pass, and he eventually puts his spare key in the door, then unlocks it. When he steps in and notices how trashed the place is, annoyance rolls off him.

"What the hell?" Tyler asks, kicking a beer can before seeing the empty tequila bottle on the counter. "What the actual fuck?" His voice raises an octave when he finally sees the bare ass on the couch. "Everleigh!" Tyler yells. The naked guy doesn't move, and I halfway wonder if he's still breathing. Eventually, he rolls over with a grunt, reaching for the blanket that's on the back.

"Everleigh!" Tyler repeats, beating on the wall, and I assume her room is on the other side.

A few moments later, the door swings open, and she saunters out with messy blond hair in a top knot. She still has on her makeup from last night, and her mascara has slightly run. It takes everything I have not to smirk at her. If being a hot mess was a person, she'd be it.

"Can I help you?" she finally says, placing a hand on her hip. "Because you're screamin' my name like you're payin' my rent. And I don't even need to mention that judgy-ass look on your face."

His nostrils flare, and she releases an amused laugh. The sound is warm and contagious, something I'd like to hear again. "So, you must be the famous Archer I've been hearing my brother talk about so much." She holds out her hand, and I give her a shake, but her fingers linger a few seconds longer.

"Yeah," I say, meeting her crystal blue eyes. There's a flicker behind them, and I notice her brow slightly ticks up. Electricity radiates from her in ways I can't explain. At that very moment, I see exactly what Tyler was talking about when he said she's flirty. Doesn't help one bit that she's fine as hell too.

"Nice to meet you, roomie." A grin sweeps across her gorgeous face.

"Everleigh!" Tyler snaps. "You knew we were coming today. What the hell!" He holds out his hand and points at the man on the couch.

"*Why are you yelling*? No one else seems to have a problem with anything that's going on here other than you." She looks at me, almost urging me with her gaze to agree, but I'm staying neutral in this argument.

The last thing I want to do is piss off my best friend or my new roommate. I don't have a dog in this sibling fight. As soon as the thought hits my brain, a cute fluffy white dog comes prancing out of Everleigh's room. Immediately, the little furball runs over to me, the tags on her collar dangling.

"Oh, meet Sassy. She's every bit of her namesake," Everleigh admits as she sashays to the kitchen to grab a bottle of water from the fridge.

"What breed is she?" I ask to keep the conversation flowing that doesn't involve more shouting.

"An American Eskimo."

I bend down and pet Sassy's head. "Hey there. Are you a good girl?"

"I can be…when I *want*. But usually, I'm *really, really* bad," Everleigh answers, and Tyler whips his head toward her.

"Stop it right now," he demands.

"Stop what?" She winks and plays dumb, chugging her water.

I'd be lying if I didn't think it was sexy as hell, but Tyler's right about not crossing any lines. Everleigh's off-limits, and it needs to stay that way, even if she might be my greatest temptation.

Seconds later, the naked dude pushes himself up on the couch.

"Yo." He gives Tyler a head nod before walking to the bathroom and has zero fucks that his dick was out.

Everleigh shrugs, then grinds some coffee beans. She's unfazed while Tyler is ready to explode. I look back and forth between them, noticing their dynamic and thinking how strange of a first impression this has been. I don't know if living with her is the best or worst idea Tyler has ever had.

I guess only time will tell.

CHAPTER TWO

EVERLEIGH

"YOUR PLACE IS TRASHED," Tyler continues, grabbing an armful of empty beer cans from the coffee table now that the random guy is no longer there.

"I mean, if you want to clean up, go for it. Not gonna stop you, but I'm not paying for your services either," I tell him, chugging more water. I drank way too much last night, but I'm a grown-ass woman, so I refuse to apologize for living my life how I want.

Tyler rolls his eyes.

"Don't forget what yesterday was. You should be impressed that I even came home."

"I just thought you'd be more *responsible* since..." He glances toward Archer.

"I'm thirty-three, Tyler," I remind him. "I can do whatever and *whoever* the hell I want. You need to go ahead and give up the ghost on that."

Seconds later, the toilet flushes, and the guy I brought home last night stumbles back to the living room. He picks up his clothes from the floor, almost falling over as he puts one foot in his jeans.

"Jared, right?" I ask.

"Jacob," he corrects, zipping and buttoning his pants.

"Oh yeah. Okay. Well, thanks for a fun night. I'll call you later."

He gives me a head nod before searching for his keys. "Shit."

"You can go look in my room," I offer as I put food in Sassy's fancy sterling silver dog bowl.

Sassy immediately leaves Archer's side and prances over. I bend down to pet her, wishing my booty call would hurry the hell up and leave. I can tell how uncomfortable Tyler and Archer are. My brother's always been protective of me, but at my age, he's more like an overbearing dad. I put the ground Colombian coffee beans in my coffeemaker, then press start. Right now, I need something strong and dark, and for once, it's not a man.

"Found 'em," Jacob eventually calls out. When he returns to the living room, I notice the purple hickeys on his neck. Except I'm not the *only* one who does.

Tyler grinds his teeth when Jacob walks over and tries to give me a kiss on the mouth. Before our lips can touch, I quickly turn my head, so my cheek takes the brunt.

"See ya soon, baby," he purrs, and I realize in this lighting how dirty those shots of tequila did me. The guy isn't my type, but it's not like I slept with him with the intent to marry him. I just wanted to have a good time. Gemma did try to text some sense into me, but her warnings not to do anything stupid apparently didn't work.

As my brother crosses his arms over his chest, I somewhat

wished I'd had listened to her. Then again, what's done is done.

Jacob lingers as if he's waiting for me to agree. "I think it's time for you to go," I bluntly say since he's oblivious of the awkwardness that's swallowing me whole.

"Oh right," he says, looking at my brother and Archer as if they magically appeared. I let out a breath when he finally leaves.

"I can't fucking believe this. You didn't even know his name?" Tyler questions in a snappy, judgy tone. My head pounds, and I just want this coffee to finish brewing so I can drink it, then sit in the tub for an hour.

"Meh." I shrug. "Not sure what the big deal is."

"The deal is you're acting like a player."

"I didn't choose this life. It chose me," I taunt, aware it'll irritate him more, though I don't give two shits what he thinks about my personal life. The last thing I want is to be berated in front of Archer, who's actively avoiding eye contact with me. Once the coffee finishes, I pour a cup, then add sugar and creamer.

"Want some?" I ask Archer, grabbing another mug from the cabinet.

"Sure," he says, but I'd already started filling it full.

He takes a few steps toward me, and I smell the light hint of his cologne.

"Help yourself to the cream and sugar."

"Thanks, but I like it plain." He sips it, and his eyes go wide. "That's strong enough to put hair on your chest."

A small smile hits Tyler's lips. "Better than that instant shit, isn't it?"

"You want some?" I glance at him.

He shakes his head. "I'm good."

I meet Archer's gaze. "You ready for the big house tour?"

Swiping away loose strands of hair that have fallen from my bun, I'm somewhat embarrassed by the first impression I've given him. Tyler's need to call me out for it hasn't helped.

"Yeah, that'd be great," he says.

With a smile, I lead him to his room. Since I knew he was coming today, I made sure to change the sheets and wash the comforter. I also moved all my spare clothes out of the closet so he'd have more room. Though I don't think he brought much with him.

Archer looks around, but I can't quite read him.

"Is it okay?"

He turns with a perfect smile and kind eyes. "It's amazing."

"It's not a huge room, but…"

"It's more than enough. Thank you," he says genuinely.

"I'm happy to help. You're a dog person, right?" I ask when Sassy saunters in and jumps on the bed.

Archer chuckles. "I can be."

I lead him to the main bathroom, and he peeks inside. "There are two in the house. This one only has a shower, but the master suite has a tub, and if you ever wanna use it, go ahead."

"Great, thanks," he says.

"And this is the laundry room."

Archer scans over my scattered dirty clothes on the floor.

"Sorry for the mess," I admit. "I'll try to be a bit more tidy since you're here."

"Everleigh," he says. I love the sound of my name rolling off his tongue. "It's not a big deal. I was in prison for five years. Seriously, this is already a million times better. Even with a naked dude on the couch."

That has me laughing hard, which only makes my head pound more, but at least he sees the humor in all of this. "Well, I'm glad I haven't made you want to run away yet. So some ground rules…." I say, moving back to the living room.

"Oh, Tyler already laid some of those down."

"Did he?" I pop a brow, watching Tyler clean the mess in the kitchen.

"Yep. I sure did," he admits, and I roll my eyes at his fatherly tone.

"I'm sure they're nothing like *my* rules." I give Archer a wink.

A smirk meets his lips, and I can only imagine what my brother has said about me. I halfway wonder if Archer got the same "off-limits" talk as I did. Tyler drove it home that I wasn't to lead Archer on, sleep with him, or flirt with him. I explained that flirting was a hard limit of mine and laughed it off. As I've told him a million times before, I do *whatever* I want.

I glare at Tyler, then meet Archer's chestnut brown eyes again. "Well, my rules are simple. Clean up after yourself. Treat Sassy like the queen she is and take her out if you can. She gets fed twice a day and gets treats after she goes potty. I like to spoil my sweet little baby." I bend down as Sassy runs over, then starts jumping and licking my face. "Yes, you are my sweet baby girl."

Tyler rolls his eyes.

"Hey, don't even. She slept in your bed when you lived here, and you spoiled her more than I did!"

He laughs. "Maybe, but I don't let her lick me in the mouth. That's just gross."

I keep my comments to myself and turn to Archer. "Want to see my room now? It's where all the magic happens."

Tyler nearly chokes as I lead Archer past him. If my brother wants to push my buttons, I'll make sure to return the favor.

"Excuse the mess. I really like clothes and shoes," I tell him as he follows me to my bathroom. "The tub's pretty great after a long day at work. I can only imagine how much of a hard-ass your boss is gonna be."

"I heard that!" Tyler shouts from the kitchen. I can hear a ball bouncing, followed by Sassy's nails tapping across the hardwood floor. The fact that he's playing with her makes me smile, especially since he tries to act like such a hard-ass all the time.

After Tyler has nearly cleaned up my entire house and taken out the trash, he checks the time and tells me he needs to get going.

"You gonna be okay here by yourself with her?" he asks Archer, but I'm not entirely sure if he's joking.

"He will be *just* fine, big brother. I don't bite that hard." I smirk, because my brother's about to pop a blood vessel.

Tyler looks at Archer. "Call me if she gets out of hand and you need to be rescued."

"You act like I'm going to make an Archer voodoo doll or something. We'll be just fine," I reply, then face my new roommate. "I'll show you my doll of Tyler later."

Archer chuckles, clearly amused by our antics, but Tyler is less than impressed.

"Remember what I said," he warns me, and I wave him off.

"I'll be here at six to pick you up in the mornin'."

"Sounds good. Thanks again for everything," Archer tells him.

"You're welcome. Bye, y'all. Stay out of trouble, *Everleigh*."

"Pfft." I turn on my heels and grab some meds for my headache.

Once Tyler is gone, I let out a relieved breath. "Well, now that Buzz Killington is gone, are you hungry?"

"I'm okay. You've already done so much for me."

"Nonsense. I'm starving, so I'm gonna make some avocado toast. It's not a big deal to make you some too."

"Uh, sure. Never had that before, but I'm willing to try anything once."

I look over my shoulder at him as I pull the ingredients from the fridge. "Awesome. It's actually my specialty. Has had men beggin' for another night."

He ignores the last comment. "So you like to cook?"

This question makes me snort. "Not really. I can make a few key things, but usually, it's a frozen meal or a sandwich. Easy stuff."

"That actually doesn't sound so bad."

I meet his eyes and see the same broken expression I saw on Tyler's face when he was released. Archer's mysterious and polite, and I'm drawn to him in a way I've never really experienced before. I have this urge to protect him at all costs, though he probably doesn't need it.

"Do you like to cook?" I pull out the bread and throw two slices in the toaster.

He chuckles, and I love the way it sounds. "I'm probably rusty now, but I enjoyed it at one point in my life. My mom loved to cook, and it's how we bonded when I was a kid. But those times were few and far between before I moved out."

"My mother was useless, so consider yourself lucky you got that much," I blurt out, though I'm positive Tyler told him all about our childhood. "What was your favorite thing to cook?"

22

"Meatballs with a homemade marinara sauce," he responds quickly.

"Ooh, that sounds delicious. I love Italian food, especially with wine. Maybe you can make it for me one day?" I can feel Archer's eyes on me as I peel, then mash the avocado onto the toast.

"Sure, I'll have to see if I can remember the recipe for the meatballs."

"If not, I can always help you find a new one," I offer, then crack the eggs into the hot, buttery skillet. Honestly, I think these are the most perfect sunny-side ups that I've ever made, and when I slide what I prepared in front of him, I can tell he's impressed. The black cracked pepper just adds a special touch.

"Damn. These make me feel like royalty." His eyes widen as he grins. "Thank you."

It makes me smile as I sit in front of him at the breakfast bar. We eat in silence for a while, and it feels nice and normal. I want to learn every single detail about him and his past, but it's important I give him space right now. The last thing I want to do is bombard him with a million questions. So instead, I say nothing at all. I'll wait until he's ready to talk about it.

When Archer finishes eating, I fill my mug to the top as he rinses our plates.

"Thanks again for allowing me to stay here. I'll try to stay out of the way, so you won't even know I'm around."

"Don't be silly. Roam around naked if you want," I tease. "Plus, if my brother trusts you to live with me, then I do too, Archer. He said you were like family, and that's enough for me."

"Means a lot," he says, then goes to his room. A part of me wants to follow him to make sure he settles in okay, but I don't want to come across too pushy.

Tyler may have warned me to stay away, but I didn't realize how hard it'd be when Archer Boone is so damn sexy and mysterious.

CHAPTER THREE

ARCHER

THE FOLLOWING morning doesn't come as early as I expect it to, considering I struggled to fall asleep. It's hard to comprehend that I'm free to do whatever I want, but it's even harder to break out of a schedule I've had—meals and falling asleep at specific times—for the past five years. Though the accommodations were awful, it always takes me a bit to get used to a new place.

After I shower, I dress in a pair of jeans and a T-shirt. I didn't bring much with me, but I'll eventually buy more clothes once I make some money.

I walk into the kitchen where Everleigh's making food. She looks gorgeous with her blond hair pulled halfway up to reveal the softness of her neck. It's hard for me not to focus on her ruby-red lips when she smiles and shows off her perfectly straight teeth. My roommate that I'm looking at is not the hot mess I was introduced to yesterday.

"Mornin'," she says, taking a sip of coffee. "Made you some toast with grape jelly."

"That's sweet of you. Thank you."

She pops an eyebrow, noticing the way I'm studying her. "What? You have a look on your face. Spill it."

"Are you always so…" I try to search for the correct word. "Observant?" The last thing I want to do is tell her how absolutely fucking gorgeous she is, considering we just met.

"Yes." She snorts. "I'm good at reading people. So what is it? Did you sleep okay?"

"Yes, just fine. And nothing really. I'm just not used to someone taking care of me. I was always the one who took care of everyone."

"Well, get used to it," she says as she hands me a cup of coffee, then joins me at the breakfast bar.

"You're going to spoil me if you keep this up," I tell her, though I truly do appreciate how much she's trying to make me feel at home.

A laugh escapes her. "Good. Means you'll live with me longer."

I find it easy to chat with her about absolutely nothing. "What time do you have to be at work?" I ask.

"Oh, I'm going in at seven, but the boutique doesn't open until nine. I have some new items I need to put out, and I'm trying to get ahead with decorating the shop. I'm sure Tyler's already warned you about my Christmas obsession."

I nod. "He showed me what the front of your boutique looks like now too. Very festive."

"Right! It looks like it was decorated by the fall queen, doesn't it?" She beams with pride, which makes me smile.

"Yes. Something like that."

"Well, just wait until Santa Claus comes to town." She waggles her brows. "Faux snow, reindeer, and presents. I can't wait to display it all."

26

"I'm sure your customers love it," I say, and she agrees with a nod.

As soon as I finish my breakfast and look at the time, I hear a car door shut outside. I'm not sure Tyler has a late bone in his body. A few knocks ring out, and Everleigh answers it, allowing him inside.

"You clean up nice," he tells her.

"Of course I do," she throws back.

"Mornin'," I say, chugging the rest of my coffee because it's too good to pour out.

"Good mornin'. Ya ready?" He looks around the spotless house but doesn't say anything.

"Want some coffee?" Everleigh offers just as Sassy runs toward him.

"My sweet girl," Tyler says, bending down to pet her. "No, thanks. I had a cup already."

"Wanna take her outside?" Everleigh asks. "She's already gone once, but she'd probably go again."

"Sure. But quickly 'cause we gotta get goin'," he says, then leads Sassy to the back door to go outside.

Everleigh's standing so close to me that I can smell the faint hint of her floral perfume. When her arm brushes against mine, electricity streams between us, and it nearly knocks me down. I'm convinced she feels it too.

Her eyebrow perks up, but thankfully, Tyler returns. He looks at us standing close to each other and narrows his eyes at Everleigh.

"You ready?" I ask, putting much-needed space between us.

"Yep," he says, giving Sassy one last pet before telling Everleigh goodbye.

"See y'all later. Try not to bore Archer to death."

"Yeah, yeah," Tyler responds.

We walk to his car and get in. There's a car seat in the back, and I still can't believe he has a baby. We used to talk a lot about what our futures would look like, and I'm happy he got exactly what he wished for.

"First up is the DMV since it's a thirty-minute drive. The doors open at seven, but it's best to get there before the rush. Afterward, we'll hit the post office and bank. Then I'll give you a tour of the gym," he says, pulling out of the driveway.

"Sounds like a solid plan," I admit. These tasks are daunting for most people, but it means ultimate freedom to me.

It takes a few hours for us to get everything done, and I had almost forgotten how impatient people can be while waiting. Couldn't imagine any of them being behind bars for five years.

After I get a license with my new address and open a checking account, relief washes over me.

After the bank, Tyler puts the car into drive, and we head to the gym. "Oh, tomorrow I have to meet my parole officer at eight."

"Ya need a ride?" he asks, and the guilt begins to pour in because the last thing I want is to inconvenience him even more. He's already driving me all over today.

"Nah, I don't want to be a burden. I'll order a taxi or something."

"You kiddin' me? You aren't, not even close. I want to help you, Archer. That's why I told you to come out here. Trust me, I'm more than happy to do whatever you need."

"Thanks, man. I just feel…I don't know. I can't really explain it."

"You don't have to. I understand, and I'm here for you, man. Please don't ever forget that."

I nod, grateful to have a friend like Tyler.

Once he parks, we walk to the entrance. The place is larger than I imagined, and I love the oversized windows across the front that give a perfect street view.

Once I step in, I'm even more impressed than I already was. The first thing I notice is the juice bar along with all the equipment.

"Want to try one?" Tyler asks.

"Sure. I can't remember the last time I had a smoothie."

"Oh, you haven't ever *had* a smoothie until you've tasted one of these." Tyler smirks.

A younger woman who looks like she recently graduated high school is running the bar. There are a lot of options, and I can't decide what I want.

"What's your favorite?" I ask her and look down at her name tag. Raquel.

"Well, I really like the pumpkin cream or the classic strawberry banana."

"Surprise me," I say, and within a couple of minutes, she's sliding a pink concoction across the countertop. I take a sip, and my tastebuds nearly explode in my mouth. "*Wow.*"

"Right!" Tyler eagerly nods as he leads me to the section of free weights and exercise machines. "We're so damn busy during lunch because everyone wants smoothies and protein blends."

"That's awesome for you guys," I add, nearly inhaling the magical drink in my hand.

"Yeah, it is. Really grateful." Tyler waves a hand around the room. "This is the main area where people work out," he explains before leading me to a secluded area.

"This is what I couldn't wait to show you." There's a boxing ring and kickboxing bags with gloves and powder sitting against the wall. For the first time in years, I feel like I'm where I'm supposed to be.

I'm speechless as I take it all in.

"Incredible, isn't it?"

"Hell yeah, it is! I can't believe you have a full-sized ring in here." I move forward, running my hand across the posts and ropes.

"Want to put on some gloves?" He walks over and grabs two pairs. "You have to put your weight on the floor and feel the bounce."

I slip the gloves over my hands and swallow down my emotions. Boxing was one of the only things that saved me when I felt like I had nothing else in life. When we were cellmates, Tyler taught me everything he knew, and considering I wasn't as experienced, it gave me something to look forward to. Throwing punches the correct way and learning how to read my opponent helped me so damn much.

I had a lot of internal anger to work through, and boxing helped with that.

Tyler puts on his gloves, and we step into the ring.

"Go easy on me. I haven't boxed with someone else in a while," I admit as he positions himself.

We throw a few jabs, and duck then punch, connecting with his cheek. The motion of it feels incredible. After a few staggered steps, Tyler laughs and connects with my jaw. After we've both taken a few hits, we come to a truce and call it quits.

"You've gotten faster on your feet, and your posture was perfect," Tyler compliments.

"Thanks. I kept training after you left. Gave me something to focus on," I admit.

"Which is exactly why I'd like you to start training others. We have a long-ass waiting list right now, and we can barely keep up with it. Of course, I'd start you off with some beginners who have no clue what they're doing, but pretty soon, you'll have more experience than me."

"Really? You think I'm ready for that?"

"More than ready, Archer. You've been working on this for years."

"Wow, I'm honored. I honestly would've cleaned the toilets if that's what you needed."

He pats my back. "And let all that talent go to waste? Hell no. This will be good for both of us. I'm glad you're here."

I nod with a grin. "Me too."

"I was thinking next week you could start shadowing one of our other boxing coaches, Matt. He'll be here in about thirty minutes."

"Sounds like a solid plan," I say as Tyler leads me to the locker room that has a steam room and hot tub. After the tour, a muscular guy with broad shoulders enters.

"Matt," Tyler calls out. "This is Archer."

"Hey, man. Nice to meet you." He shakes my hand with a firm grip. "You're the boxer, right?"

I give him a curt nod. "Yep, that's me."

"Heard good things about ya." His client walks in, and Matt excuses himself.

While I fill out my employment paperwork, Tyler answers a few membership questions from some locals. Once we're both finished, he turns to me. "Wanna go out for lunch?"

"Sure," I tell him, and we walk outside. After a few

minutes, we cross an intersection and arrive at a building that looks like it was built in the 1950s.

"This is downtown in all its glory," Tyler says.

I chuckle. "This is it? You said small town, but this is tiny."

As soon as we enter, a bell dings above the door, and we're quickly greeted by an older woman.

"Hey, Tyler," she says, squeezing him tightly. "And Archer!"

She pulls me in next as if she's known me my whole life. "We're huggers 'round here. It's nice to meet ya. I'm Belinda."

"Oh yeah, Tyler told me about you. Nice to meet you too."

"Hopefully all good things." She winks and grabs two menus.

"It was!" Tyler confirms as she leads us over to a booth by the window.

"Today's special is cowboy chili. Since the temperatures are startin' to drop, it's the perfect dish for fall," she says. "Coffee?"

Tyler nods.

"Same for me."

"Got it." Belinda walks away with a hop in her step.

"She's pretty awesome. You'll probably see a lot of her since she's dating Gemma's dad," he tells me, just before she returns with two steaming mugs.

"You're comin' to Thanksgiving dinner on Thursday, right?" Belinda asks and notices my reaction, then turns to Tyler. "You haven't invited him yet?"

He chuckles. "I was gettin' to it. Gemma reminded me before I left this morning too."

I speak up. "I'd like that. Thanks."

Belinda instantly smiles again. "Good. You're too cute to be sittin' at home alone. Plus, I love to cook. Speakin' of, do y'all know what you're havin' today?"

"I think I'm going with the special. Add onions and cheese, please," Tyler says.

"Same," I tell her.

"Great choice! It'll be right up." She turns and walks away.

"Sorry I didn't mention Thanksgiving dinner earlier. It's gonna be great, though. Belinda's an excellent cook and loves to feed us. I've had to run several extra miles a week because of her."

"She's got spunk. I like her already." I pick up my coffee and blow on it.

"Oh, just wait until you meet Gemma's dad," he says. "Jerry's her perfect match."

"I'm sure he is."

"So, are you excited to start trainin'?"

"Hell yeah! I can't wait. Seriously."

"Having you at the gym is gonna make things so much better. I have a feelin' our memberships are gonna spike." Tyler flashes me a smirk.

I chuckle at what he's implying. "Thanks, Tyler. I hope it does," I say.

CHAPTER FOUR

EVERLEIGH

SINCE IT'S the day before Thanksgiving, I know it's going to be a busy one. The boutique is having a huge Black Friday sale this weekend, and I'll be getting ready for it. Christmas is my favorite holiday, so I'll be going all out with decorations per my tradition. I even wore my *Hallmark Christmas Movies and Hot Cocoa Weather* sweater. Although Christmas was hardly celebrated when I was a child—mostly because my alcoholic mother couldn't save enough money for gifts or food to save her ass—I've made up for it as an adult by going to the extreme. By the end of the night, Ever After will be glowing in white lights with red and gold garland.

I take Sassy out the back door and inhale the fresh, crisp air. It's around sixty degrees, and I'm living for it. Though I'm a Southern girl through and through, I love it when it's cool enough to snuggle up with a blanket and some hot cocoa. Sassy, on the other hand, doesn't appreciate it. She quickly pees, then scurries back inside.

"You're such a diva." I laugh as she sprints to the couch.

Checking to make sure I unplugged my curling iron and

turned off all the lights, I go through my mental tasks list for the day. I'm so deep in my head, I don't see Archer come out of his room until I nearly run into his solid chest.

"Shit, sorry." I stumble back before I knock him over. "I'm still waking up, apparently."

"Don't worry about it. My eyelids are barely open." He yawns, and when my gaze lowers down his body, I find his happy trail pointing at his morning wood. Archer's boxers hang low on his waist, and it's not hard to notice how fit he is. His chest and arms are covered in tattoos, and he has a nipple piercing.

"You're allowed to have that in prison?" I ask, staring awkwardly at the silver hoop I want to lick.

He blinks, then meets my stare with a slanted grin. "No. Not really."

"Oh. I like it. Suits your whole bad-boy vibe."

"Thanks, I guess."

Fuck, I'm making him uncomfortable. It's barely been forty-eight hours since we met, and I'm already gawking like he's a piece of fresh meat.

"Well, I'm off to work. If you're able, will you take Sassy out around lunch? I normally come home and do it on my break, but—"

"Yeah, not a problem. I think she's getting used to me."

We both turn toward a growling Sassy, and I snort. "Feed her treats, and she'll be your best friend in no time."

He scrubs his fingers through his short, dark hair. "Noted. Maybe I'll spend a few hours trying to befriend a dog."

I shrug with a grin. "Not a bad way to spend a day if you ask me. There's plenty of food in the fridge and pantry, so help yourself."

"As soon as I get my first paycheck, I promise to pitch in

for groceries and bills." His expression drops, and humiliation spreads over his face.

Instinctively, I reach out and grab his arm. "Please don't worry about that. You're my brother's best friend. I'm happy to help."

He tilts his head to where my hand is wrapped around his bicep, and I quickly remove it. God, I'm making him feel right at home with my awkward touchiness.

"You have no idea how much I appreciate it, Everleigh. But I will help as soon as I'm able."

The way my name rolls off his tongue sends shivers down my already heated body. I grin, hoping to ease his concerns. "I'll tell Tyler to pay you extra so you can buy us a steak dinner. He owes me one anyway." I flash him a smirk, and the corner of his lips tilts up just the slightest.

"Sounds good. Can't remember the last time I had a decent slab of meat."

"Ironically, me either," I joke and smile wider when his cheeks redden. Considering he saw a naked man on my couch two nights ago, he's probably putting the pieces together that he was a bad lay.

"Sorry to hear that." He avoids my gaze like he's trying to hold back laughter.

I'm aware that I can be a bit much for some people. Blunt, outgoing, feisty when I need to be—but I think he's more amused by me than anything.

"Alright, well I better go if I'm gonna make coffee before I leave."

He gives me a nod, then turns toward the bathroom. My eyes lower to his ass. Or rather his *dump truck* of a booty. His chest and stomach are lean, but his back muscles, arms, and everything lower provide a *very* pleasant view. I wouldn't mind nibbling on every inch of him.

With that thought, Archer looks over his shoulder and catches me staring. I quickly snap my eyes to his with an innocent expression. Without saying a word, I turn on my heels and go to the kitchen to fill my tumbler.

Just as I'm throwing my oversized purse in my car, I notice a sleek black Escalade parked outside my house. My neighbors drive minivans or big-ass Ford trucks—so it stands out like a sore thumb. But if I *had* to guess, Carley, the single mom across the street, must've let her Tinder date stay overnight. Not that she's said as much, but it's one of the rumors floating around. One of the many benefits of owning a boutique is always hearing the latest small-town gossip from the customers.

I drive the short distance downtown, park, then grab my stuff. As soon as I unlock the doors, I flick on the lights and smile. This store is my happy place, and outside of my home, there's nowhere else I'd rather be.

"Good mornin'," Lexie sing-songs as she prances in thirty minutes later. She's one of my managers, but we've become close friends too.

"Morning!" I reply cheerfully from the front display I'm organizing. "How's it goin'?"

"Just fine, I suppose. Brett's mama asked if I could make a pecan pie for Thanksgiving, so I'm stressin' about that."

"Why? Just go to the bakery and pick one up," I suggest with a laugh.

"No way. She'd know I didn't bake it and give me one of her signature *I'm not mad, I'm just disappointed* looks. Then she'd make some offhand comment to Brett about how it's too bad he didn't marry a woman who's skilled in the bedroom *and* kitchen."

37

"She'd say that?"

"Oh, that'd be on the list of *nice* things she'd say about me." She huffs, then grabs our daily task list.

"Wow. So glad I don't have to put up with a villain mother-in-law. But I like to think I'd win her over with my sailor's mouth and Southern charm."

"You better pray yours isn't the devil dressed in a pantsuit."

At that, I snort. "Not sure I'll ever be gettin' married, so I won't have to worry about that."

"Why do you say that? Thought you'd already be engaged to your roommate by the way you've been talkin' about him the past few weeks."

I bark out a laugh because she's right. Since Gemma mentioned him moving in with me, I've randomly brought him up in passing. I wasn't sure what he looked like, but when we finally met a few days ago, he surpassed every expectation I had.

"He's been quiet. We've only talked a little, though when I ran into him before work, I'm certain he caught me checking out his ass. Per usual, I made things weird with inappropriate gawking and stupid words."

"Most guys like that about you," she retorts with a smirk.

"No, they like my long blond hair and lean legs," I correct with a shrug.

"It's been less than a week, right? He'll come around and realize you're funny as hell."

"Then he won't be able to stay away…" I mock, waggling my brows. "I'll break him out of his shell in no time."

"Didn't you say your brother invoked a hands-off policy?" she asks.

"He thinks he's the boss of me, but he's not."

"Careful, Ev. Archer was locked up for five years. He probably needs to figure out a lot of stuff before he can consider a relationship."

"Geez, you sound just like Tyler now. And who said anything about a relationship?"

"Oh, so just fuck buddies? Friends with benefits?" she prompts.

"Roommates with benefits," I counter with a chuckle.

"Not sure if I should warn Archer or rat you out to Tyler first," she taunts.

"Better not. I sign your paychecks."

"Yeah, yeah," she grumbles but grins.

"I'm taking him to Thanksgiving tomorrow. We're all going to Gemma and Noah's father's house. Belinda's cooking, so it'll be a good opportunity for him to hang out and lower his guard."

With those words, the door chimes, and our first customer of the day enters. Between helping people, decorating, and getting all the Black Friday signs hung, the day stays busy.

When I leave, it's almost dark. As I pull onto the main road toward the grocery store, I see the same black Escalade parked outside the boutique. It's probably someone's family visiting for the holidays and spending the evening shopping downtown.

Belinda is preparing a feast for us tomorrow, and I've offered to bring my infamous dessert. I only bake it a few times a year and look forward to it each time. On a whim, I stop and pick up a couple of steaks. After chatting with Archer this morning, I realized he probably hasn't eaten a decent meal in years. While I'm no Chef Ramsay, I can make meat and potatoes.

Sassy barks the second I walk into the house. My arms are filled with grocery bags, so I can't pet her.

"Chill, girl. Let me set these down before you bite my ankles off."

As soon as I kick the front door shut, Archer's in front of me, grabbing the bags from my grip.

"Let me help."

"Oh. Thanks. In the kitchen's fine," I say, tossing off my heels.

"I know where it all goes," he tells me.

I mentally slap myself for insinuating he wouldn't.

"Hope you're hungry," I say as I unpack everything.

"Sure, I could eat." He flashes a boyish grin. "Can I help?"

Before I can answer, Sassy's at my side, begging for attention. I set the steaks on the counter, then lean down to pet her.

"Were you a good girl today?"

"Only nipped at me three times," Archer responds. "Better than the five yesterday."

I try to hold back a laugh but fail. "With that progression, she'll be your bestie in about two days."

"You bought ribeyes?" he asks, eyeing the items I haven't put away yet.

"Yep. Hope you like baked potatoes and sweet corn. Went to the store for cake ingredients and came out with a week's worth of stuff."

"I do, but you didn't have to do that for me."

I lift my head and meet his eyes. "Would you rather watch me eat instead? I heard some guys are into that fetish…"

He scratches his cheek. "Hm, yeah. Tyler warned me you were a smart-ass."

I smile widely at the compliment and playfully poke his shoulder. "And it'd be best if you didn't forget it."

After I ask him what temperature he'd like his steak, I get to work in the kitchen. An hour later, we're both full and satisfied from the impromptu feast I made. We talked some while we ate, but he's guarded with his past. I don't push him and am okay with what he's comfortable sharing.

"That was the best meal I've ever had," he tells me as he rinses the dishes.

"Wait till you taste my dessert."

"W-What?"

"Oh my God, that sounded way more sexual than it should've. I meant the cake I'm baking for tomorrow."

He fights a smirk. "What kind?"

I lick my lips, then grin. "Better than Sex cake."

He stares at me for a minute, probably waiting to see if I'm messing with him, but I just grin. "Trust me. You'll orgasm before you swallow the first bite."

Archer watches and listens as I ramble on about random small-town gossip while I mix the ingredients. He probably doesn't care that much, but he humors me.

Once I place the pan in the oven, I clean up, but Archer quickly jumps to his feet and grabs the bowl. "Let me do that for you."

His hands cover mine, and I swallow hard before meeting his eyes. "You don't have to."

"Let me. I feel useless otherwise."

"Alright." I release my grip, then fill the bowl with utensils.

He sets it in the sink and fills it with water. I wipe the counter, and Archer gently takes my wrist. "Stop. Go sit."

I contemplate arguing but decide against it. "I'm not used to having help, so you'll have to forgive me," I tell him.

41

He drops my arm and smirks. "Well as long as I'm here, you don't have to do everything. I've spent years feeling like a burden. Plus, I like having things to do."

"I'm sure Tyler will keep you plenty busy at the gym." I grab my wineglass and refill it. Taking a sip, I happily watch the show in front of me.

Archer's biceps tense under his sleeves, and it's hard not to imagine him manhandling me in bed. Veins pop down his forearms to his hands, and I wonder how it'd feel to have his fingers wrapped around my throat.

"*Everleigh?*"

I blink to clear my inappropriate thoughts. "I'm sorry. What?"

"I asked where your dishwasher detergent was."

"Oh, sorry. Um…left cabinet underneath the sink."

Archer continues cleaning in silence as I drink my wine and admire him. Tyler demanded I stay away from Archer, and that's not fair.

Especially since I'm already tempted as hell to break all the rules.

The following morning, I wake up and immediately smell

hazelnut brewed coffee. It takes me a second to remember that I didn't set the timer. I open my door and scan the living room. My gaze lands on a shirtless Archer opening the fridge and pulling out the bottle of creamer. Sassy watches him with amazement as she sits and drools over the view. *Same, girl, same.*

"Mornin'," I say, walking closer.

He spins around and *fuck me* if my eyes don't land on the appendage between his legs that's currently saluting me.

"Good morning. Since you made coffee yesterday, I figured I would today."

"Wow…um…thank you. Smells delicious."

"You want this flavor? Vanilla?" He holds up the bottle.

"Yes, please. Just a little."

He stirs it in, then hands me the mug.

I smile graciously. "Thank you. Do you drink coffee?"

"Yes, but just black. None of that sugary shit."

"Hey." I scowl. "That sugary shit is what gets me through the day."

"Really? Not a morning person then?"

"Actually, I am, mostly because of work. Just takes me a bit to wake up. I love staying up late and binge-watching TV or going out, but either way, I'll always need my coffee."

He chuckles when I release a loud moan with my first sip. "Duly noted. Keep you caffeinated."

"And fed," I add. "I tend to get hangry when I haven't eaten."

"Well, then I better get ready so we make it to Jerry's on time." He pierces me with his gaze after he catches me staring at his package again.

I blink and swallow down the hot liquid. "Oh, right. I gotta hop in the shower. Unless you wanna go first."

"I can shower after you."

I take another large gulp of coffee, hoping the warmth will calm the ache between my thighs. Once I've emptied my mug, I set it in the sink. "Or we could conserve water and take one together," I sing-song over my shoulder.

Archer's lips twitch as he tries to suppress a laugh, and I swear his cheeks redden just a little. "I'll just wait till you're done."

"No fun," I tsk.

After I finish, Archer makes us some eggs, and we watch the last half of the Macy's Thanksgiving Day parade. By noon, we arrive with my Better than Sex cake in hand. I can tell he's nervous, but I'm determined to make sure he's comfortable and has a good time. As soon as we walk in, everyone bombards us.

"Hey!" Gemma wraps her arms around me as Tyler gives Archer a bro hug.

Tyler introduces him to those who haven't met him yet. Jerry's rocking Scarlett in his arms, and Gemma still has her new mama glow, which I love seeing on her.

"The babies are here!" I gush when I spot Noah and Katie. "Can I hold them?"

"Of course, take your pick," Katie teases. She has one, and Belinda's got the other.

"Not mine. We're besties now," Belinda states.

"You have to share," Owen chimes in. He's Katie's eleven-year-old son. "That's what Mom tells me anyway."

We laugh at his eye roll. I adore how much he already loves being a big brother.

I take one of the boys from Katie and softly rub the pad of my finger over his soft cheek. "What's his name?" Archer leans over and asks.

"Uh…Finn. Wait. Luke." I squint, trying to figure out which one I have. "Well, I have a fifty-fifty chance of being right."

"That's Finn," Katie corrects. "Luke has a little mole above his lip."

"Ah, yes. I knew there was something like that."

"He's so tiny," Archer says.

"They're less than a week old," I tell him. "Isn't he precious?"

"When they're sleeping," Noah interjects. "Otherwise, one needs to be changed at the same time one wants the boob. Then they switch places."

"That's how newborns work, Daddy," I tease him, then face Archer. "He's a new father, can ya tell?"

"I basically raised my little sister, but I can't say I'd ever be fully prepared for babies. Yours look pretty sweet, though." Archer looks around, and his expression tightens. I can tell he didn't mean to share that with everyone.

"Alright, kids. The turkey and fixin's are ready. Find a seat," Belinda announces, handing Luke over to Noah while Jerry gives Scarlett to Gemma.

"I can hold my niece while you eat," I offer, handing Finn back to Katie so she can re-swaddle him.

"Oh no, I've mastered eating one-handed now." Gemma waves me off.

"Oh come on, you're just afraid I'm going to tell her all your secrets and where to buy the cheapest alcohol," I taunt as we make our way to the dining room and sit.

"I take it you're the cool aunt, huh?" Archer smirks as I sit next to him.

"Damn straight. Coolest aunt, coolest sister, coolest friend. You're all welcome, by the way," I beam.

Once Jerry carves the turkey, we say grace and dig in. Owen talks about baseball while I make silly faces at Scarlett from across the table.

"So, I heard you had quite the birthday," Katie says. "Sad I missed it."

"Heard the morning after was the real party," Gemma teases.

"Ha-ha. I had to drink for both of you since you didn't come."

"I was giving birth." Katie snorts.

"I passed out by eight. Trust me, I wouldn't have been good company," Gemma says. "Between midnight pumping and getting up to take Owen to school, I'm a walkin', talkin' zombie until bedtime."

"Aren't you glad you're rooming with the fun one?" I say to Archer.

"You don't have to comment," Tyler interjects. "I'm looking high and low for another place for you."

"Hey! I take offense to that." I scowl. "Sassy's new daddy and I have a good thing going. Don't be a homewrecker."

Gemma bursts out laughing, knowing damn well my brother's about to pop a blood vessel. And I swear I hear Archer choke on his food.

"Yeah, I'm sure he enjoyed seeing your date on the couch in *his* birthday suit," Tyler throws back.

"He wasn't my *date*…and it was a special occasion. I drank more than usual, so sue me." I shrug.

"I'm fine staying there," Archer chimes in. "I've gotten used to Sassy barging into my room at six in the morning, and I've finally figured out the coffee maker, so it can only go up from here."

"See?" I wave a hand. "We're doing great."

"Oh right, shoulda warned you about that damn prissy dog. Never let me sleep in when I lived there." Tyler shakes his head.

"Stop worryin', big brother." I dramatically grab Archer's hand so everyone can see. "We're gonna be one big happy family!"

I glance at Archer, who's more amused than anything. Luckily, he doesn't scare easily and tends to go with the flow.

While I know he needs time to adjust, I have a feeling my head and body are going to struggle to keep my distance.

CHAPTER FIVE

ARCHER

SITTING with Tyler's friends and family is surreal.

I've never experienced a real Thanksgiving dinner, not even as a child, and being here makes me feel included for the first time in my life. *A family.*

I could get used to this.

However, the guilt of not being with my sister eats at me. I wish I lived closer to Annie and Sadie, but I didn't want to be a burden. I would've had to sleep on her couch and didn't have a job lined up there. I'm grateful to Tyler and Everleigh for giving me the tools to start over.

"Where'd you live before?" Owen speaks up over the chaos. "Before you lived with Aunt Everleigh?"

She's not really his aunt, but I think it's cute, considering how close they all are.

Everyone stops talking and looks at him, then at me.

"Um...I lived in Nevada."

"Did you not like it there? Is that why you moved here?" he asks.

"No, I didn't like it," I offer.

"Do you have any siblings?"

"I do. A younger sister named Annie. And a niece. Sadie's five."

"Are they in Nevada?"

"No, she moved to Wyoming before Sadie was born."

"Oh. Did you get to see her a lot?"

"Owen, sweetie…" Katie grabs his attention, but I don't mind the questions. "Do you want more turkey?"

"No thanks." He re-directs his focus back on me, and I stifle a laugh. Owen's a curious one.

"She'd come and visit me once a month," I tell him. "So, I got to see Sadie, and then we'd talk on the phone once a week."

"Will they come visit you here?" he asks, shoving a forkful of potatoes in his mouth.

"I hope so, eventually."

"How much younger is Annie?" Gemma asks.

"Three years. Just turned thirty," I respond.

One of the twin babies starts crying, so Katie excuses herself. Noah follows as they go to where they'd been sleeping.

"So if she's thirty, that makes you thirty-three," Everleigh says. "You're the same age as me."

"So, are you a Scorpio or Sagittarius?" I ask.

"Scorpio, but I'm right on the border, so I identify with both signs." She grins. "What's your sign?"

"Aquarius."

"Oh my God. You're one of my matches!"

"Excuse me?" I ask.

"Sagittarius and Aquarius are compatible signs. Like soul mates," she explains.

Tyler coughs, clearly uncomfortable, which causes me to

chuckle. Belinda changes the subject and asks me how I like Lawton Ridge.

"So far, so good. Haven't been out much, but I'm excited to be involved at the gym. Working out has been something I've always enjoyed. I'm looking forward to training and teaching others how to box too."

"Could you teach me?" Owen asks.

I look around, unsure how to respond, but decide to nod. "If your parents say it's okay, sure."

"Cool." He grins wide.

"How come you never asked me?" Tyler acts insulted. "I own the gym, ya know."

Owen shrugs as if he doesn't want to hurt Tyler's feelings.

"It's the tattoos, isn't it?" Everleigh teases Owen. "They make him look badass, amiright?"

"Ev…" Katie shoots her a glare as she returns with a baby in her arms. "*Language.*"

"Mom, it's okay. The babies don't understand bad words," Owen innocently explains, and everyone bursts out laughing.

We finish eating, and most of us are groaning about how full we are. But I can't deny my desire to try Everleigh's cake.

"Belinda, that was absolutely delicious," Gemma says, and we agree in unison.

"Sure was," Jerry says, kissing her cheek.

"Thank you for letting me join you," I say. "Even though I'm basically a stranger."

"Oh, don't be silly. You're one of our kids now," Jerry states.

I can't hold back my gratitude. He has no idea what that means to me. My own father didn't even want me around.

"Thank you. I appreciate being included."

Everleigh stands and grabs her plate, and I do the same.

Together, we clear the table while the others chat. Tyler meets me in the kitchen, carrying more dishes.

"How ya holdin' up?" he asks.

"Just fine. Better than my previous accommodations." I chuckle.

"You mean I only have to provide better housing than a prison cell?" Everleigh taunts. "Hope I've exceeded all your expectations."

"You were in prison?" Owen gasps from the doorway.

Shit.

I'm not sure how much he knows about Tyler and Noah being in prison too, so I stay quiet.

"Owen, sweetie. Let's go check on your brothers. I think I hear Finn crying," Everleigh says, guiding him back toward the dining room.

"Guess I should anticipate that reaction," I mumble when it's only Tyler and me.

"It gets easier." He shrugs. "People will talk. You can't stop that, but you also didn't do what you went there for. Just gotta shake it off."

Easier said than done, but I don't tell him that.

"I'm glad you're fitting in with everyone. I was hesitant to have you live with my sister, but I see y'all are getting along just fine."

"Yeah, we are. I can't imagine rooming with anyone else," I say with a grin, not giving any more details. Everleigh's a spitfire with high energy and a bubbly personality, which is opposite from me, but she's entertaining nonetheless. I already see myself liking her more than I should. Right now, I'm forcing myself to only think of her as a roommate and friend.

"Alright, who's ready for my Better than S—"

"Cuddling," Katie quickly interrupts as Everleigh brings it

to the table. Katie gives her a look and nods her head toward Owen.

Everleigh forces a smile. "Better than Cuddling cake, yes."

"What's in it?" Jerry asks.

"Chocolate, caramel, and toffee." She places it down. "With whipped cream and chopped candies on top."

"Oh my God…" Noah groans with a smirk. "I wish I would've saved more room."

"Especially since you have to wait five more weeks…to *cuddle*," Everleigh taunts, and the room fills with laughter.

"If he's lucky…I'm thinking longer," Katie deadpans.

Noah's brows rise. "Excuse me, woman?"

"Yeah, right. You two could hardly keep your hands off each other. Pretty sure that's how she got knocked up in the first place," Everleigh blurts out, then realizes Owen's hanging on to her every word.

"Forget I said that," she tells him.

After everyone has a piece, we dive in. It's, in fact, the best dessert we've ever had, something we all agree on.

"Don't eat too much. I still need models for the boutique," Everleigh says, directing her attention to Tyler and Gemma. "Assuming you're not game?" she asks Katie.

"Not unless it's for post-maternity moumous."

"How'd I get roped into this?" Tyler asks. "Is it an athletic line, at least? Because I could support that."

"No, but you're my brother, and I need some male models since I'm adding a men's line. Nice jeans, shirts, ties, and shoes. You look good all dressed up," she tells him.

"I'll do it as long as you don't make me wear anything too tight," Gemma says. "I have ten pounds of baby weight I still need to lose."

"You're crazy, but fine. I have some cute winter dresses I can put you in." Everleigh shrugs.

"What about Archer?" Gemma suggests, and every set of eyes is on me as I stuff cake in my mouth.

"Yes...he'd sell your entire collection in a heartbeat with his tats," Katie agrees.

"Especially since he gives off the whole bad-boy vibe," Gemma adds.

Tyler and Noah give their wives a look of disapproval, and I hold back a grin.

"What?" Gemma and Katie say in unison.

"That's actually not a bad idea..." Everleigh arches her brow as she scans down my body. She reaches over and squeezes my arm. "Good biceps. Sexy smile. Intense brown eyes. Maybe a little hair trim and you'd be the best eye candy in the state."

"Y'all are critiquing him like a piece of meat," Tyler says.

"Don't be jealous, brother," Everleigh taunts, and he rolls his eyes.

"Well, what do you say, Archer? Can I get you naked?"

I nearly choke on my dessert. If I looked at Tyler right now, I'm sure he'd be sporting a disapproving scowl, so I don't.

"To dress you in my clothing line, of course," she emphasizes, enjoying catching people off guard.

"Considering you're letting me invade your space, I'd be happy to help," I say honestly. Though I've never modeled before, I can't deny the excitement I feel at spending more time with Everleigh outside of the house.

"Yay! You can even keep a few outfits. They'll look great on you in case you need them for a night out or something."

"Especially if he has a date," Noah says. "As soon as chicks

53

see him at the gym, I have a feeling membership numbers are gonna climb."

I stiffen and wait for Everleigh's smart-ass remark, but she stays silent.

Clearing my throat, I speak up. "Nah, I have no plans on dating anytime soon. Gonna focus on getting clients and working." I promised Everleigh I'd pitch in as soon as I got paid, and I plan to keep my word.

"I'll be your first client!" Owen announces.

I flash him a wink. "Thanks, buddy."

Belinda talks about some of the stories she's heard at the deli recently while I continue eating. It's weird to know personal details about people in this town I haven't even met.

After a while, the babies get fussy, and everyone decides it's time to leave. Belinda takes me by surprise when she gives me a big hug and invites me to come have lunch at her deli again.

"Will do, ma'am," I tell her.

"You gotta try the upside down turkey and gravy sandwich," Everleigh suggests.

"You gonna join me?" I ask.

She looks at me with a smile. "Yeah, it'll be a date!"

Everleigh drives us back to her house and immediately takes Sassy for a walk. The dog nearly leaps out the door and looks like she's walking Everleigh instead. It causes me to laugh as she runs to keep up. Perhaps I should try walking the little shit.

I change into some joggers and a black T-shirt. Just as I'm settling on the couch, my phone rings, and I smile when I see my sister's name on the screen.

"Hey, sis." I answer the FaceTime call. "Happy Thanksgiving."

"Hey, brother."

"Uncle Archer!" Sadie hops onto Annie's lap.

"Hey, kiddo! Did you eat some turkey?"

"Yep! And mashed taters, gravy, and corn. Mom made me eat veggies too." She sticks out her tongue.

I chuckle just as Everleigh returns with Sassy. She notices my phone and pinches her lips. However, Sassy doesn't get the memo and begins barking at me.

"Do you have a dog?" Sadie squeals in excitement.

"My roommate does. Wanna see?"

"Yes!"

I flip the camera around and face Sassy, who's sitting at my feet, glaring at me.

"She's so cute! I want a puppy, but Mom said no."

"I said not right now," she corrects. "Not while we're in an apartment."

Sadie's shoulders sag, and I wish I could help them get a house. Something bigger and with a yard.

Everleigh comes into view and gives my niece a little wave. "That's Everleigh, Tyler's sister."

"Oh, she's pretty," Sadie says nice and loud. "Is she your girlfriend?"

Everleigh grins, and it's obvious she overheard.

"No, we're friends," I say awkwardly because...are we friends? Or just roommates?

"But you live together?" Sadie gives me a look, and Annie's just seconds away from sending her off.

"Yeah, but we have our own rooms," I try to explain.

"Why don't you get ready for your bath so I can talk to Uncle Archer for a minute," Annie tells her.

"I'll talk to you soon, kiddo. Make sure to call me later, okay?"

She blows me a big kiss. "I will! Bye!"

Annie sighs and waits until Sadie's out of earshot. "How was your Thanksgiving?"

"Great. Tyler and Everleigh invited me to lunch with their friends, and I ate my weight in turkey and cake."

"Cake? No pie?"

I chuckle. "Nah, Everleigh was in charge of the dessert and made Better than Cuddling cake."

Everleigh cough-laughs from somewhere in the kitchen, and it's obvious she's listening.

"Is that a Southern recipe?" Annie asks as I try to hold back my amusement.

"You could say that." I shrug.

We chat for a few more minutes until Sadie returns and says she's ready to get in the tub. I tell them goodbye and that I love them before hanging up.

"Your niece sounds adorable," Everleigh says when I open the fridge. "Sorry, I wasn't trying to eavesdrop."

"No, it's fine. Sadie's loud like her mother, so it's impossible not to hear her." I take out a bottle of water.

"I bet you miss them being far away."

"I do, but then again, I'm kinda used to it. I hate that I

wasn't around when Sadie was born and only got to see her during their monthly visits. It's all she knows of me, and I hope to change that eventually."

"Should have them come visit. They're more than welcome to stay here. I can get an air mattress and make room for them in the living room. Could have one big slumber party." She leans against the counter and smiles genuinely. When she crosses her arms, the movement lifts her breast, and I find myself lowering my gaze, then quickly meeting her eyes.

"I bet they'd love that," I say. "But I don't want to put you out even more than I already have."

"Archer." Her voice lowers, and it's obvious she's being serious. "This is your home now. At least that's how you should think of it."

Reluctantly, I nod, shoving my hands in my pockets. "I'm trying. It's a big adjustment for me."

Pushing off the counter, she walks closer, causing my heart rate to increase. She's so damn beautiful, I have to remind myself not to stare like a creep.

"Would it help if I slapped you around a bit?" She playfully punches my arm. "I assumed you and Tyler got into some fistfights being around each other all the time. When he'd bother the hell out of me, I always got the urge." She laughs, and it makes me laugh too.

"Only when we were boxing or working out," I admit. "He actually taught me a lot."

I'm not sure how much of my past Everleigh knows, and although I'm tempted to share some of it with her, I don't. The last thing I want is for her to regret letting me live here or think the worst of me. Whatever Tyler decided to tell her will have to be enough for now.

"Yeah, he's pretty good at that. Maybe I'll join Owen and come kick your ass someday."

Now that has me howling. "You're half my size, but I'm up for the challenge."

"Are you saying I'm too small to defend myself?" She acts like she's insulted.

"No, but the thought of you trying to take me down makes me wonder if I should be locking my bedroom door at night."

She backs up a little, glaring at me. "You should. You *really* should, Archer Boone."

Her taunting voice has me fighting back a smile.

CHAPTER SIX

EVERLEIGH

"Ouch," I groan as I soak in the tub and rub the bottoms of my feet. My body feels like it's been hit by a dump truck. Black Friday at the boutique was a madhouse, and Saturday was just as busy. We opened early, stayed late, and I don't think I took a lunch break on either day. The shelves need to be restocked since every holiday item sold out. Thankfully, I have more inventory arriving first thing tomorrow.

My customers were so excited that they lined up along the sidewalk beginning at four in the morning. I overbought with hopes to sell out, and it actually happened.

The only thing I missed was not seeing Archer that much. When I finally got home, we ate dinner, then passed out.

After I'm out of the bath, I put on some jeans and an oversized sweater. Today, Archer and Gemma are modeling the new items I'm launching this week. Thankfully, Lexie and Dana are working today, so I have plenty of time to take photos. I can't wait to post the pictures of Archer in the new clothes because with his good looks, tattoos, and golden-brown eyes, selling them won't be an issue.

I never planned on carrying a men's clothing line until my customers asked, well *begged*. They wanted to buy them for their husbands, sons, and grandsons, so I looked into it after being asked for months.

There's already a men's store in town, but they only have basic things like fire-proof jeans and fishing shirts. I've researched all the new trends in men's fashion, and Lawton Ridge isn't gonna know what hit them when I launch, especially since I have a secret weapon—my new roomie, Archer Boone.

It's just past ten, and I've been up for a couple of hours doing laundry and cleaning up around the house. I asked Gemma to meet me at eleven, and considering she's just as punctual as my brother, I need to get going. I go into the living room and find Archer on the couch. He looks up at me with a boyish grin. I love it when his gaze slides up and down my body.

"Wow, you look nice. That color really suits you," he says.

"Thanks. It's called holly berry." My cheeks heat to the same color as my sweater. Not wanting him to notice, I move into the kitchen to grab some water. "Are you ready?"

"Absolutely. I already took Sassy out too. And fed her again," he admits.

I give him a look. "You're gonna fatten her up, and then she won't fit into her doggy sweaters."

He chuckles with a shrug. "She looked hungry."

"She'll give you those begging eyes even when she's full. Sassy played you big time!"

As soon as I say her name, she jumps up on the couch and rests her head on his lap. "Told you it wouldn't take long for her to warm up to you."

Archer pets her and tries to get up so we can leave, but

Sassy's dead weight.

"Wanna treat?" I bribe. Once the magic word is spoken, she immediately makes her way to the kitchen. I pull some bacon treats from the bag and give her some commands to sit and shake. Archer stands and stretches, allowing his shirt to ride up. After catching a glimpse of his abs, I turn and grab my keys before he notices.

As we're pulling out of the driveway, he seems nervous. "Today's gonna be fine. I promise."

"I'm sure it will. I'm just not used to…the attention."

I glance over at him and smile. "I'm happy to help debut you to the world."

"That sounds absolutely terrifying." He chuckles.

We park a block away from the shop because the lot is full. Before I unbuckle, Gemma pulls in behind us. "I knew she was gonna be here thirty minutes early!"

When we get out of the car, Gemma greets us. She looks amazing with glammed makeup and perfectly curled hair. Not a strand is out of place.

"Damn, woman. Aren't you a reminder of exactly why my brother married and knocked you up?"

She snorts and flips her hair. "You're damn right. Guess I still got it."

Archer laughs. "Tyler was always obsessed with you, and I don't think that's ever gonna change."

"Oh, it won't. He can't keep his hands off me. I mean, at this rate, I'm gonna be pregnant for the next decade."

"I'm not complainin'," I tell her. "Gimme all the nieces and nephews because I'm not getting pregnant for a *loooong* time."

"You don't want kids of your own?" Archer carefully asks, and I find it sweet how gentle his words are. He seems sensitive to those things, maybe because of his sister and how close he is with her. One thing I can say, the man knows how to respect women, something I'm not always used to. Just like that, Archer checks another box on my *Husband Wish List*.

He hurries to add, "I'm not trying to pry. My sister thought since she had endometriosis, she'd never get pregnant, but she did. The doctors aren't always right."

My face softens when I meet his eyes. "No, it's nothing like that. It's just best to be in a solid relationship before you start having babies. Single moms are rock stars, but it'd be really hard with my business, so I've always tried to be super careful. Also, I don't want to raise a kid in the same shitty toxic environment that I grew up in. I want them to have parents who actually *want* to be involved in their life. It was a promise I made to myself when I was younger. I refuse to repeat the cycle."

"I can completely understand that," he says, and there's a moment of unspoken words.

Gemma walks in step beside me. "Reason number 5,784 why you need to find a nice Southern gentleman to settle down with to have some cute babies. You gonna let Katie and Noah give me all the nieces and nephews?"

I loop my arm in hers. "Yep. And if she keeps spitting out more than one at a time, you'll have nothing to complain about. Keep it up, Katie!" I shout into the air with a fist pump.

Gemma sticks out her bottom lip. "It's not for me. It's for Scarlett! She needs some cousins. So, have babies for her."

"…to babysit!" I continue her sentence.

"You better not wait that long!" Gemma scolds.

"Gives me a good what? Sixteen years? Also, I can't believe you're begging me to get knocked up. I'm not the *settling down type*." I use air quotes.

She lets out a sigh. "You're right. I swear you think more

like a man than an actual man."

I waggle my brows at her. "I'm a *man*eater."

Archer snorts but doesn't say anything. He probably thinks I'm crazy.

As soon as I open the door to the boutique, several of my regulars greet me as we make our way through the crowd. Now that the church services are over, the place is packed. When we pass the singing Santa display, he immediately starts his ho ho ho's as Christmas carols blast through the speakers. Now, I realize adding five gigantic Christmas trees full of ornaments throughout the shop might not have been the best idea. But they're gorgeous nevertheless.

"Oh, sorry, dear," Mrs. Jefferson says as she bumps into me. "Also, I heard from a little birdie that you might launch something new this week."

"You know I like to keep it secret."

"As long as it involves him, I don't think it matters."

She's obviously flirting with Archer even though she's twice his age. Her husband passed away last year, and now she's single and ready to mingle—her words, not mine. She even told me about how I should use dating apps like her to find a nice young man.

Gemma leans in closer. "Could probably dress him in women's clothes at this point, and they'd sell."

"Right!"

"I heard that," he mumbles.

We continue to the storage room in the back. Dana and Heidi pop in to say hello but then immediately go back to helping customers. They're my part-time employees and have been working for me for over a year now.

I place clothes in their sizes on two separate racks. "I want you in this first," I tell Gemma, pointing at the outfit.

"Yeah, yeah. I know the drill," she says. Considering I've asked her to help with nearly every launch I've done, she's a pro.

"This is your first one," I tell Archer, directing him to the employee bathrooms.

While they're changing, I put fresh batteries and a memory card in my camera. As soon as I'm set, they return.

"Wow! Absolutely perfect." I can't stop smiling at how good they look. Archer looks better than I imagined. "Outside we go."

I want to take full advantage of the sunlight splashing against the brick wall so I lead them to the back of the building. Gemma moves into place, wearing a baggy maroon sweater and winter leggings. She accessorized the scarf with her hooped earrings flawlessly.

"Gorgeous."

Since she doesn't need much guidance, I move around her, getting different angles. "Make love to the camera."

Her head falls back with laughter, and I snap the shot. After I've gotten plenty of that outfit, she changes into the next one.

"Yes, girl! That turtleneck dress is so going home with you today. Lord!" I adjust the long gold necklace making sure the layers are seen, and then we get started again.

I make Archer pose with Gemma some too. Eventually, she makes it through all her outfits.

"Ready for your solo debut?" I ask Archer, nodding my head toward the brick wall.

"I dunno. Gemma's a hard act to follow." He grins.

She shrugs. "I think I was a model in my past life."

"Pfft. You're a model in *this* life. Do you have any idea how many people ask for your contact info after I post your pics on

Instagram? I mean, I proudly tell them you're currently in a modeling contract and are unavailable."

"A contract, huh?"

"Yes, with me, *for life*." I laugh. "I'm not sharing your beauty with any of these other boutiques. I found you first, and you're mine. Plus, you married my brother, so you're legally committed to me."

"Ha-ha, okay, deal." She wraps her arms around me and squeezes.

"Okay, okay, now I gotta get to work!"

Archer stands against the wall like a statue. Before I take any pictures, I lower the camera and stare at him. "You look like you're plotting a bank robbery or doing calculus in your head. So which is it?"

A small smile plays on his beautiful lips, and it's exactly what I wanted. While I continue coaching him, I can't help but be mesmerized by his soft brown eyes.

He turns his body, and the sleeve of the jacket wrinkles, so I move forward to fix it. At one point, we're so close, his warm breath brushes against my skin, causing butterflies to swarm.

"Those jeans look great on you, Archer," Gemma compliments. They're acid wash and fit him like a glove. I stand back and take more pictures.

"You should take off the jacket," I instruct. He's wearing a black collared shirt with silver buttons that shine in the sunlight. Needing to style it a little better, I adjust it.

Carefully, I roll the sleeves up to his forearm and ask him to do the other one but keep his hand there for the shot. Once I'm back in place, I can't press the button fast enough. "Bite your bottom lip a little."

He laughs, but I'm not kidding. These clothes are going to fly off the shelf because these pictures are hot as hell.

"Okay, go ahead and take off the shirt."

His eyes widen. "And change?"

"No, no, no. Just take it off and show me those muscles you're hidin'," I say confidently.

Hesitantly, he reaches for the top button, and I'm so damn anxious watching the shirt slide off his shoulders.

As I stare at him, I'm tempted as fuck to lick his abs. Gemma walks over and grabs the shirt, and even I see the way her eyes linger for a beat.

"Now *that's* gonna sell some jeans," I blurt out at seeing his tattoos on full display.

Gemma's phone rings, and she walks off to answer it, which gives me time to compose myself.

"Did you put on the boxers?" I ask.

Archer's brow cocks up. "Yes."

"How about you pop that top button then and show off the band."

Archer licks his lips, his voice as smooth as velvet. "You didn't tell me I'd be half-naked."

"You'll be half-naked," I deadpan. His gaze pierces through me, nearly pinning me in place. If he only knew the things I'd do to him if he'd let me.

Gemma returns and breaks the trance I was in. "Everleigh likes to leave out important details like that. Don't worry, you'll get used to it and learn to ask the right questions next time."

"Next time?" Archer arches a brow, then undoes the top button and slowly unzips the jeans. I wait with bated breath as he reveals the black band of the boxers. My mouth goes dry as I study his happy trail that goes beneath his clothes. I take so many pictures, I lose count.

"Okay, I think we're good. Costume change!"

Archer goes inside, and Gemma glares at me.

"What?" I ask innocently.

She flashes a devious grin. "I saw that. You two were basically eye-fucking each other."

"I'd do more than eye-fucking if my brother hadn't given me a stern talkin'-to," I admit, wishing my body hadn't given me away. If Gemma noticed, I'm sure Archer did too.

"Yeah, he's been adamant about that for weeks. I think he's just worried about you," she reassures me.

"When will he stop with the overly protective big brother thing?"

Her face softens. "Probably never."

"I love Tyler, and I know he means well, but give a girl a bone."

"A real-life bone," she adds just as Archer returns.

"Okay, I'm ready," Archer states, seeming more comfortable in the black slacks, belt, tie, and cream dress shirt.

Lowering my eyes down his body, I say, "Damn, I think I'm pretty good at this outfit thing."

"I'd say so," Archer agrees, adjusting the black tie that pops against his shirt.

I notice the hem of one leg is tucked into his dress shoe. "I like this pose, so don't move an inch."

I hand Gemma my camera and move toward him. I drop down to fix the material, and when I glance up, our eyes meet. Heat rushes through me again, and my heart rate increases as I think about how close I am to his cock—that just so happens to be bulging against the slacks.

I gulp hard when his brow arches as if he's noticed my reaction. When I stand and turn around, I meet Gemma's eyes. Immediately, she starts taking photos.

"You two get together?" She points her finger at us.

"*Gemma...*" I say. My panties are soaked, and being this close to him is tempting enough.

"Nope, time for you to give the camera some *action*."

I snort at her choice of words but don't argue, even though I never post pictures of myself online. I'd much rather be the one behind the camera.

However, I humor her and pose next to him as she clicks away. Archer pulls me closer, grasping my waist with his strong hands as we stare at the camera.

"Wow, Ev. You're a natural. Why aren't you modeling your own clothes?"

All I can do is laugh.

Archer's hand slides down, brushes across my ass, and slips into my back pocket. Goddamn, the man is such a tease. There's no way he can't feel the electricity between us right now.

Gemma continues snapping pictures, and when she lowers it, I move forward to grab it. "Welp, guess I need to get goin'. Time sure does fly!" A sly smile meets her lips as she hands me the camera.

I give her an evil look because it's more than obvious what she's doing.

She gives me a hug and whispers in my ear, "Your brother may be against it, but I'm all about that happily *ever after*. Especially if it gives me a niece or nephew."

Grinning, I squeeze her tighter and thank her again.

"Nice seein' you, Archer. Don't be a stranger," she says with a wink.

"You too. I'm sure we'll see each other again soon," he responds.

When we're alone, he looks at me. "Shall I go change?"

"Yeah, that's a good idea. Don't want to lose the good

natural lighting."

When he walks back into the shop, I try to compose myself. I need to be professional, but Archer ignites something in me I haven't felt before.

When he returns, I brush hair out of my face and grin. This time, he's wearing dark wash jeans and a navy tee. Between his muscular arms and tats, the gossip mill is gonna lose their shit. Luckily, he seems to be growing more relaxed with each passing second.

Once these are posted, I'm going to get a ton of comments and messages asking about his relationship status, and my jealousy won't be able to handle it. Of course we're only roommates, but if anyone is getting a chance to be with him, it will be me. I'll elbow a bitch to be first in line.

"We're almost done here," I tell him as I move around and click more photos.

"Whew, okay," I breathe out. "I think we're good. Wanna see?"

He nods and comes closer as I scroll through them.

"Wow, they look great. You got some good angles."

"Really?" My voice goes up an octave because hearing his approval sends shivers down my spine.

"Yeah, photography is definitely your thing."

I shake my head. "Nah. I just learned how to do this because of the shop. Trial and error. Kinda figured it out and taught myself what works and doesn't."

I keep sifting through them until I find the ones Gemma took of us. Stealing a sideways glance, I see his mouth move into a small smirk.

I wish I could read his mind so I could learn everything about him and his life before coming here, but I'd still rather hear it from him.

After Archer has changed into his own clothes, he comes out and tries to hand me the hangers, but I shake my head. "Those are yours."

"Everleigh," he prompts.

"It's my way of saying thank you. They looked amazing on you. Perfect for a date."

I swear I see his eyes darken a shade. "I'm not going on any dates unless you're talking about the one at the deli you promised me."

"Oh, right," I say as he opens the back door of the shop for me.

"Y'all rocked that rush," I tell my employees as I meet them up front.

All three of them are working today because we've been super busy since Black Friday.

"I'll see y'all tomorrow," I say with a wave, then lead Archer outside.

"So, was today everything you expected?"

He grins, walking beside me. "Didn't realize I had 'showing you my underwear' on my bingo card, but here we are."

"Better get used to expecting the unexpected with me," I tease, though I'm being serious. As we get closer to my car, I see the same Escalade parked across the street. My eyes focus on it as concern washes through me.

"What's wrong?" Archer asks when he notices my demeanor change.

"Did you see that black SUV?" I ask after I start the engine. He nods. "Yeah, why?"

"It's probably nothing, but I just keep seeing it parked around town. It's odd because I know what everyone drives here, and I'm pretty sure whoever it is, isn't a local."

He scratches his cheek, then glances over his shoulder to look at it. As soon as he does, the Escalade makes a U-turn, then speeds off.

"Maybe they just moved here, and it's someone new in town?"

"Hmm, you could be right. I think I'm just paranoid after what happened with Tyler and Noah."

"Possibly. Or maybe it's a serial killer." He flashes me a grin, which causes me to laugh.

"Thanks, that makes me feel a lot better," I deadpan.

Archer laughs, and it warms my heart to hear his deep baritone.

Once we're home and inside, I take Sassy out, then grab my laptop from my room. I get cozy on the couch and load the photos into my editing software.

Archer scoots closer beside me, peeking at my screen.

I brighten some, soften others, and do some cropping so they fit nicely on my Instagram page.

"Wow," he mutters. "They were good before, but now they look super professional."

"Once I post these, prepare for *a lot* of attention." I glance at him.

That same heated gaze from earlier returns, and I'm tempted to kiss him just to see what he does.

"Anyone can look like that when they're dressed and posed by a pro."

I suck in a deep breath and purposely zoom in on his abs.

"Clothes don't create this." Moving the mouse around, I go to his biceps. "Or this." Then I zoom into his seductive eyes. "I'm literally gonna have to lock you in my house." I chuckle.

"I've been locked up long enough."

My smile fades at the realization of my stupid comment,

71

and I mentally berate myself. "Oh my God, I'm sorry. I didn't mean it like that."

"Though if I could choose to be a prisoner to anyone..." He lingers with a sexy-ass smirk, and my bottom lip falls into my mouth. "Being yours wouldn't be so bad."

Fuck. Now I really want to make a move to see how he'd react.

Before I can do anything, Sassy jumps up next to Archer and steals his attention away.

"You're a sweetheart, aren't you?" he coos, petting her.

Sassy looks up at him with big puppy dog eyes, and it makes me snort.

"I think she's adopted you into our family now."

He continues petting her, then turns toward me with a somber look. "Sometimes, I think about prison and try to find something positive from it, so then I'm not so resentful."

"And have you?"

"Yeah," he says with a smile. "Meeting your brother changed my life for the better."

"I'm glad you did because without him, you wouldn't be sitting next to me."

"And there's no one else I'd rather be rooming with. Even though the circumstances that brought me here are sucky, I'm grateful for what I have now—a nice place to live, a good job, and my very own pooch."

I gasp when Sassy pushes herself into his lap. "Excuse me, show him who your mama is!"

She puts her paw on Archer's arm.

"You traitor." I scowl, but then laugh at how cute they look together. If I have to share Sassy with anyone, I'm glad it's Archer.

CHAPTER SEVEN

ARCHER

EVERLEIGH'S LAUNCHING her new items at nine today. When she asked me to model, I hadn't known what to expect, but I actually had fun with her and Gemma. I can't deny the way she makes me feel. Deep inside, I want to give her everything her longing gaze begs for, but I can't.

One thing about that day has been bothering me— the way Everleigh reacted to seeing that black SUV. After I've had a few days to think about it, I wonder if it's someone from my past. Based on the numerous letters Chad's family sent to the judge, they weren't happy I was getting out early on parole. They're the only ones who'd have the nerve to come for me. Well, more specifically, his sister, Krystal. She's always been crazy and couldn't accept that her brother was the abusive one in the relationship.

After finishing with my first client, Toby, I go to the juice bar for a protein shake. My muscles are sore from the lifting I've been doing after my shifts. I have full access to use the facility when I want, and it's been a nice outlet. Working out has also helped keep my mind off Everleigh. She's sneaking her way into my everyday thoughts even though I've been trying hard to ignore them.

"Hey! How's it goin'?" Tyler greets me as Raquel hands me my drink. It's just the pick-me-up I need.

"Good. Toby's really enthusiastic about training. Nice to have someone who loves it so much already."

"Yeah, he is. Lookin' forward to seeing where he goes with it. He's got the strength, just needs the guidance."

"Absolutely."

"Did you see Everleigh posted the pics?"

"No, haven't had a chance to yet."

"Gemma said she's gotten several texts already asking who you are. These women are trying to track you down. Might be good for business, though." Tyler smirks.

As soon as the words leave his mouth, two middle-aged ladies enter, and their gazes land directly on me. "Oh there he is," one purrs.

"Can I help you?" Tyler asks.

"Of course. We'd like to sign up and have him as our trainer." She points at me, flashing me a wink.

A booming laugh escapes Tyler. "I guess I spoke it into existence. Well, we can get you started, but Archer—"

"What an adorable name! My *single* daughter is—"

Tyler clears his throat and quickly interrupts. "Archer coaches boxing."

They give each other a puzzled look, then shrug. "Will it help me with self-defense?" the redhead asks.

"Well, yes," Tyler replies politely.

"Then boxing it is," she cheers.

Tyler takes them to the front counter and introduces them to Constance who helps get their paperwork started.

"You might be booked with students for the next two years."

"All who are gonna try to hook me up with their daughters and granddaughters. Something I absolutely don't want."

Unfortunately, one woman has caught my eye since I've arrived.

Tyler laughs, patting me on the back. "Might have to start paying you commission then."

We wait as they sign the contract and pay their first month. I have a feeling this is just the beginning. Being single in this town seems to be a crime, and no one's gonna be happy until you've been set up.

"So about tonight, I think I need to give you a little warning." Tyler gives me a look that implies a *big* warning.

"About decorating?" I ask, confused. Everleigh said she's putting up her Christmas decorations, but I'm not sure how that'd be a big deal.

"Yes, and I'm sure Everleigh just said you'd be putting up a tree, but it's more intense than that. Imagine the North Pole this time of year. Her house will look like that but worse. She likes to downplay things, especially if you don't know better, and leaves out the fine details. So just be aware."

Now, I'm chuckling. "I honestly expect nothing less, especially after the photo shoot when she didn't tell me I'd nearly be stripping down to my underwear. I think I have her personality pegged."

"You probably do, but I can't stress enough how crazy she gets about Christmas. I think it's because when we were kids, we didn't have huge holiday celebrations, so she's doing everything in her power to make up for it now. Ever since she got her own place, she's had a tradition every first of December.

Decorations explode throughout the house, and she bakes dozens of cookies and blasts music. Oh and you can't forget the cranberry wine. I'm sure there'll be several bottles available."

"Somehow, I have a feeling you're not joking." I can imagine Everleigh singing and dancing around, which causes me to smile.

"Nope. You'll see what I'm talkin' about soon."

"Thanks for the warning," I tell him with a smirk. "I'm sure it will be a jolly good time."

"That's one way to put it." He chuckles, then is called away by Smith, one of the guys who do monthly maintenance on the building. I go to the boxing area to wait for my second student. As soon as he shows up, we start with basic techniques, and the time passes quickly.

Eventually, my shift is over. After I disinfect everything, Tyler offers to give me a ride home. When we're in the car, I check the time and see it's just past six. Before he pulls into the driveway, I scan up and down the street for that Escalade.

"Tell her we'll be over within the hour to help. Gotta get Gemma and the baby."

"Sure will," I say, grabbing my bag.

As I'm walking up the sidewalk, I hear the music blaring and Everleigh singing at the top of her lungs. Taking a deep breath, I enter, and she rushes toward me with a wineglass. Her other hand is holding something red and green.

"Archer! I got you a Christmas sweater!" By the squeal in her voice, I can tell she's already tipsy. "You gotta wear it."

Boxes upon boxes of decorations are stacked on the floor along with a massive tree. Sassy comes trotting into the living room, and I notice she's wearing a jingle bell collar and reindeer antlers. Then I realize her sweater matches Everleigh's.

"Oh, you poor thing," I say, petting her head.

Everleigh playfully swats at me when I meet her eyes.

"So, putting this on is a requirement, I assume?"

"You bet your ass it is."

"Okay, okay. Whatever makes you happy." I shrug, aware that it's gonna look ridiculous on me.

She chugs the rest of her wine. "It'll make me the jolliest person on the planet other than, you know, Old Saint Nick."

Laughter escapes me as I go to my room and change. I shake my head when I see myself in the mirror, but I also like that she wants me to be a part of something she loves so much.

Meeting her back in the living room, she hands me a glass, and I notice she got a refill for herself. "Thanks. Oh, Tyler said they'll be here within the hour."

"Did he mention putting on his sweater too?"

"Um. Actually, no."

She cocks a brow. "He better not forget."

"I doubt Gemma will let him."

"Very true! Gemma always has my back."

"How long have you two been friends?"

Everleigh grins over the rim of her glass. "We've known each other forever. But I think we became best friends in middle school."

"That's awesome. You guys are lucky to have each other," I say. My high school friends forgot I existed as soon as I went to prison.

I take a sip, and it's so sweet, there's no way I'll be able to finish it.

"We definitely are." She smiles, then taps her finger across her ruby red lips. "What to do first? Want to help hang some mistletoe?"

"Sure. Where's it goin'?"

"Above my bedroom door." She hands it to me and points toward her room. I see a hook in place, and I assume she's hung it there for as long as she's lived here. It dangles above the doorway, and Everleigh stands next to me, then our eyes meet. The only thing that breaks our trance is Sassy whining at our feet.

"I'll take her out," I offer. "You've got to prepare for your guests."

"Ha! Thanks. A true gentleman," she says with rosy cheeks.

"Come on, girl." I lead Sassy out the back. She runs around, then does her business. When I return, I find garland spread out on the floor, different ornaments on her coffee table, and random fake branches scattered on the couch. It's amazing how much she pulled out in just a few minutes. Add in the ribbons, lights, and boxes full of God knows what and it's proof Tyler wasn't lying about this.

"Where're ya putting the tree?" I ask.

"In front of the window so everyone in the neighborhood can see it!" she exclaims, and I love how giddy she is. "One day, I'm gonna have one of those houses that you pull up to, turn to a specific radio station, and watch the lights flash to the music. I absolutely love those."

"Or at the boutique, so you can get more exposure for your business. Have signs out front with a hashtag for when they take pictures and share on social media."

"That's genius, Archer! What an amazing marketing opportunity that could be. Next year!" Her voice grows louder. "You're so helping me with it!"

I grin, but I also have no idea what I'll be doing a year from now or where I'll be living. Though I like the thought of still being here with Everleigh.

I move next to her on the floor with my wine in tow. She

hands me a ball of tangled lights as she works on another. "I probably shouldn't have thrown these in the box like this, but New Year's Day was rough."

"Do I even wanna know?"

"Trust me, you don't," she admits. "I always try to clean up. The whole 'new year, new me' vibes, but I think I was still drunk from the night before. Not sure if you noticed or not, but drunk Everleigh doesn't give a shit about anything. She's irresponsible."

A roaring laugh escapes me. "I believe that."

"It's the truth." She raises her glass and drinks. "Oh, I love this song!"

She wiggles her body, singing along to "Rockin' Around the Christmas Tree." When the song ends, a knock lightly taps on the door, causing her eyes to brighten with excitement.

She adjusts her sweater and opens the door. Chatter fills the room as Gemma enters with Scarlett in her arms.

Everleigh lets out a tiny squeal and takes her niece, placing kisses on her cheek. "My favorite little angel, and look, you all wore the sweaters I sent."

"Oh, was it optional?" Tyler teases, setting down the baby's diaper bag.

"Absolutely not!"

"He knew it was a *requirement*," Gemma says as Tyler unpacks a floor play mat and toys.

"Wine?" she asks, but they decline. "Guess it's just Archer and me tonight."

"The day I stop breastfeeding, I'm gonna drink like a sailor," Gemma admits as she takes Scarlett back and sets her on the mat.

"Oh, I'll make sure that happens," Everleigh says. "We should start the cookies! The guys can put up the tree."

She takes Gemma's arm and drags her to the kitchen as Tyler and I get to work. "It's been a while since I've done this. At least a decade," I admit.

"I honestly think this tree is as old as she is. Most modern ones come in sections, but she refuses to upgrade. Something about sentimental value." He rolls his eyes with a laugh.

"I heard that!" Everleigh shouts.

"There are colors on each of the metal ends, like this," Tyler explains as he shows me. "Each color gets a row, so match the colors and put them together."

"Okay, sounds easy enough," I say, then grab a couple of pieces and get started.

Tyler puts the base down and then builds the middle vertical structure that holds the limbs. It takes some time, but we eventually assemble it. We take a step back and look at our masterpiece.

"Fluff the branches some," Gemma instructs, and Everleigh agrees. The first batch of cookies comes out of the oven, making the house smell of sugar and cinnamon.

"How's this?" I ask once we've fluffed them.

"Perfect!" Everleigh beams.

Tyler checks on the baby, and I move back to untangle more lights. The girls don't realize how loud they're being and that I can hear their conversation.

"Have you heard anything else about Eric?" Everleigh asks Gemma as Tyler takes Scarlett and the diaper bag to Everleigh's room.

Eric is a name I'm familiar with as someone from Tyler's past. Tyler told me what happened and his connections to the mafia in Vegas, but I honestly didn't think he still spoke to any of those people, considering that's what put him in prison in the first place.

"They still don't know who murdered him, and it's been months," Gemma tells her. "But I wouldn't be surprised if you became a person of interest, considering you slept together."

Everleigh laughs it off, but I feel my body heat with jealousy.

She slept with Eric? And then he was murdered?

I wasn't aware, but I wouldn't even know how to bring it up to get the backstory. They continue chatting as Tyler returns.

"They can suspect me all they want. The only crime I'm guilty of is sleeping with a married man who didn't mention he had a wife. That is *not* my fault. "

"I didn't know, and neither did Tyler," Gemma adds.

"Don't bring me into this conversation," he sternly says. "I warned you not to get involved, especially since he was only staying here temporarily."

He gives me a look, and the message is clear.

Everleigh is off-limits.

Tyler comes over and helps me wrap the strings of white lights around the tree.

"I'm sorry to hear about Eric," I offer. "How long ago?"

"Two months. It's still being investigated. It was tragic and unexpected. I considered him a really close friend, and he helped me in a time of need."

"Sorry to hear that, man. I hope they find whoever killed him."

The room grows quiet other than "Silent Night" playing in the background.

I try to change the subject. "Should we have checked these strands first?"

"Shit." Tyler stops what he's doing and plugs them in. Thankfully, none of the bulbs are burned out.

"Whew, thank goodness."

"Come have some cookies." Everleigh waves us over with a mouthful. "They're so good!"

We go to the kitchen and find trays of gingerbread cookies along with what I think are wreaths.

"Okay, don't judge the way they look." She snickers when I eye her decorating skills.

We all snag one, and Everleigh holds her cookie in the air. "To family," she says, and we all tap them together. Though they're still warm, I nearly inhale it. When I look down at the tray, I burst into laughter.

"What?" Tyler asks.

"Do these gingerbread men have dicks?"

Everleigh smiles proudly. "I was waiting for one of you to notice!"

"Oh my God, I was too busy making the wreaths to notice," Gemma admits with laughter. "I totally didn't see their little ding-a-lings."

"Poor guy just hanging out with his junk out," I muse. Everleigh's kind eyes gaze at me, and I watch as her bottom lip gets stuck between her teeth. Her warmth radiates off her, and I can't remember the last time I felt so happy and welcomed.

After we've filled ourselves with cookies, we hang the garland, then move on to the ornaments. Everleigh has a huge Santa Claus set up in the corner of the room that sings and shakes his hips when the sensor is set off.

After a couple of hours of listening to Everleigh's Christmas playlist, Tyler and Gemma call it a night. We walk them outside and say our goodbyes. Everleigh hugs them both and kisses Scarlett, who's fast asleep.

"Now y'all go to bed at a decent time," Gemma says in a motherly tone.

"Yes, Mom." Everleigh snorts, then waves as they back out of the driveway.

I follow her inside and realize how messy the place is. "I'll help you clean up."

"Oh, thanks." She smiles, and I'm happy she's finally letting me do my part. We put away all the cookie ingredients, and each time I see the little gingerbread, I think about the little dicks she added and chuckle.

It's her sense of humor I adore the most. Not everyone is as free-spirited as Everleigh, and I love how confident and genuinely happy she is. I wish I could feel the same and hope some of that rubs off on me.

As we clean up the kitchen, we continuously bump into each other. One time, we crash so hard that I steady her to keep her from falling. I don't know if it's the alcohol or exhaustion, but I'm not complaining about the opportunity to be close to her.

She looks up at me with big blue eyes. The connection simmering between us is almost too much for me to handle. I fight the urge to pull her closer and slide my lips across hers. Resisting her is getting harder by the day.

I'm not actually sure I could handle a woman like Everleigh.

It's been five years, and though I fantasize about what it'd be like to touch her, I'd never disrespect Tyler. Everleigh deserves better than some ex-convict anyway. Someone who can give her more, and right now, that man isn't me.

CHAPTER EIGHT

EVERLEIGH

THOUGH I ENJOY BEING at the boutique any day of the week, I really love the vibe we have on Saturday mornings. The farmers' market is every weekend from eight to noon, and people shop the stores regardless of the weather to enjoy the music, food, and energy in the downtown area. It's especially fun when the holidays are near.

"Hey, Ev. Phone call for ya," Heidi says as Dana sorts through some shirts. "Be right there," I tell her. A group of ladies walks in, and I greet them, then ask Dana to help since Heidi's running the register.

I pick up the phone and am greeted by an energetic voice. "Hello! I was wondering about that male model you posted online."

My brows furrow as I wait for her to elaborate. "Yes, what about him?"

"Is he single? There were lots of comments on his pictures, but I never saw a clear answer."

Annoyance races through me, but I try to remain professional. "Sorry, but I'm not running a matchmaking service. If you have any questions about the clothes or items for sale in my store, then I'd be happy to help."

"I was just askin'." She huffs, and I grind my teeth.

"Alright, do you need any help with anything else?" I'm being overly nice at this point.

"No, but—"

"Hope you have a lovely day," I force out, then hang up.

"Do I even wanna know what that was about?" Heidi asks with humor in her voice.

"Someone asking about Archer's relationship status again. Completely out of line," I say.

"Honestly, what'd you expect by putting him on your pages? A new man in town…a young, single man at that. I'm shocked they haven't flocked to the shop waving their bare ring fingers."

"At least ten women have stopped me since last weekend to ask the same thing," Dana states as she makes her way to the counter. "And half of them were married!"

That has me laughing because it doesn't surprise me. "They were probably trying to set their granddaughters up with him," I say.

"Mindy Biltmore bought three hundred dollars' worth of men's clothes yesterday, and I damn well know she's not dating anyone. She claimed it was for her brother, but I have a feeling she was just trying to get information out of me. She just kept talking about Archer, and outside of having his name, I don't know shit about him," Dana adds.

There's no way I'm telling anyone about Archer's past, and it's no one's business anyway. I want him to trust me and feel comfortable sharing his past or secrets without worrying that it will spread around town. My employees know that he's Tyler's friend who needed a place to live until he could find his own, and that's it. He'll remain a mystery to everyone until he chooses to share more about himself.

"People are too damn nosy in this town," I grumble.

"True," Heidi states. "But I wouldn't be surprised if he doesn't stay single for long. If you're hoping to get a piece of that, you better act quick."

She and Dana chuckle softly as I give them both the evil eye. Archer's way more than eye candy, and what's even worse is he's off-limits. He's basically a carrot being dangled right in front of me—close enough to want him but just out of reach. He's been here less than two weeks, and we only see each other between our work schedules, but it's a fun time when we're together. There's way more to him than what meets the eye. I hope to dig deeper and uncover who he truly is.

The day passes quickly, and by five, I'm saying goodbye to the girls. I'm ready to take a bath, drink some wine, and lay low for the night. Hopefully with Archer.

As soon as I walk into my house, delicious aromas hit my senses. Sassy greets me, wagging her tail and licking my hand.

"Hey, sweet girl."

"You're home," Archer says from the kitchen.

"Yeah. Smells great in here," I tell him, then notice the table is set for two with wine glasses and a small vase of flowers.

Oh my God. Is he bringing a woman over?

I mean, of course he's allowed to. This is his home now too, but I'm going to awkwardly feel like a third wheel if I don't get out of here soon.

"I'll be out of your hair in less than ten minutes." I rush toward my room, but Archer comes out from behind the breakfast bar and stops me.

"Oh, you're leaving?" His brows pinch together, and when

I lower my gaze, I notice his relaxed attire—a black pair of Nike shorts and a sleeveless tee. Looks like he just got home from the gym.

"Yeah, I don't want to interrupt your date night. I'll just change and come back later. Midnight okay? Otherwise, I can—"

"Wait." Archer grabs my elbow before I can walk away and hide the redness on my cheeks. "I made dinner for you," he states, then adds, "for *us*."

I meet his brown eyes and feel stupid for assuming.

"I wanted to make you dinner as a thank you since I haven't been able to yet. I got paid and went grocery shopping."

This six-foot-something man is looking at me with so much pride for being able to buy and cook food. Years have passed since he's been able to do this. And he did it for *me*.

"Oh." I blow out a breath. "Well, that was so sweet, but you didn't have to spend your money on me."

"Don't worry, I had a few coupons." He smirks, and I snort. "Dinner will be ready in just a few."

"I'll be right back." I flash him a smile and head to my room.

After I get into some comfy clothes, I meet Archer at the table.

"Don't laugh, but I made something my gram used to make us. Then after she passed, I'd make it for Annie at least once a week. It became our comfort food."

I inhale and look at the cheese-covered dish in the pan he's holding. "What is it?"

With a smirk, he pulls out my chair, and I sit. He scoops a spoonful onto my plate.

"Tater tots?"

"Taco Tater Tot Casserole with extra black beans and cheese," he confirms, then puts some on his own.

"Oh my God." I take my first bite and moan. "This is speaking to my soul. So good." I shove another forkful into my mouth, not even caring that it's piping hot. I haven't eaten since breakfast, and I'm starving.

"I'm glad you like it. I haven't made it in a while, so I wasn't sure if I'd remember how to," Archer says, watching me.

"I think it's perfect, honestly. This is something I didn't realize I was missing out on. You're gonna be makin' me this once a week."

He releases a hearty laugh and nods. "Deal."

After I inhale two servings, I pat my stomach and groan at how much I ate. "This might be a bad idea."

"Why?" He furrows his brows as he carries our empty plates to the kitchen.

"I'm not gonna be able to fit into my jeans if you're gonna keep cookin' for me like this."

He rolls his eyes. "I doubt that. But if you want, I can use fat-free cheese next time."

"Ew, don't you dare!" I stand and grab the half-emptied pan and meet him by the counter. "If I promise to work out, will you buy the real deal?" I taunt.

The corner of Archer's lips tilts up, and I watch as he lowers his gaze down my body, then back up to my lips. "You really have nothing to worry about. But yes, I'll always buy the fatty cheese."

"You're the best roomie ever." I grin, wrapping my arms around him. I don't realize how close we are until he stiffens against me. "Did you want to watch something with me?"

"Sure. Just gonna clean up."

"Oh, let me. You cooked. I'll do it before I go to bed. It's kinda my nightly routine. Tidy up the living room, take out Sassy, run the dishwasher, then masturbate until I pass out fully satisfied."

Archer's eyes bug out, but he doesn't say anything. He not so casually clears his throat and diverts his attention.

"Alright."

"Well, sometimes I watch ASMR videos. Just depends how I'm feeling that day," I add with a grin.

"You're fucking with me, right?"

"No! ASMR videos are so relaxing. Sometimes, I watch them in the tub and wake up an hour later with wrinkly fingers."

Although that's not what he meant, seeing him squirm is worth it.

"I'm gonna wash up. You can pick the show or movie," he says, walking toward the bathroom.

"What're you in the mood for?"

"I'm afraid to even answer that," he calls out over his shoulder, causing me to laugh.

"Oh come on. Am I that predictable already?" I shout from the living room.

"Everleigh, the only predictable thing about you is how unpredictable you are."

Those words fill my chest with warmth. Archer's an onion whose layers are slowly peeling away, and I like that he's letting me in.

"Alright, what did you pick?" he asks when he returns and takes a seat next to me on the couch. I can smell his cologne, dark and sensual, mixed with whatever body wash he uses.

"*Only Murders in the Building,*" I finally reply when he catches me gawking. "It's a new show."

"Everything's new to me." He chuckles. "But let's do it."

"Martin Short and Steven Martin? Love them." He crosses his leg over the other.

"And Selena Gomez. She's a doll," I say, giving him a full rundown of Selena Gomez for the next five minutes. "An epic cast," I reiterate.

"Damn, okay." He laughs, and I click play.

"I've thought about hosting a podcast," I admit halfway through the show when the characters discuss starting one.

"Oh yeah? I could see that. You'd be good at that, always talking and having an opinion."

I pop a brow, unamused. "Really?"

"In a good way!" he exclaims quickly. "People love hearing others' thoughts and rants. Plus, you're one of those social types."

"You should do it with me then. I bet people would love to hear about your experiences."

He shrugs uncomfortably, and I mentally slap myself. Of course he wouldn't want to talk about prison.

"You could discuss being a boxing coach. Maybe find some new clients," I suggest.

"Maybe. Though I'm booked up as it is now."

"Really? That's amazing! I didn't realize that many guys around here would be into that. The ones I meet are either rednecks who live in hunting gear or twentysomethings whose mothers still wash their dirty sheets."

Archer snort-coughs as if he's trying to hold back laughter.

"Yeah, it's a real good time trying to date in small-town Alabama." I groan.

"Well, I do have a few male clients in their twenties, but I actually have more women over the age of forty who want to learn self-defense. They like the morning sessions after they've freshly showered and caked their face with makeup." He smirks.

"Oh, so you've met the cougars of Lawton Ridge," I taunt. "Surprised Tyler allowed that."

"Why? Their money's just as good as anyone else's."

I shoot him a glare. "I bet."

He snickers, and we bring our attention back to the TV. It's not until it ends that we both gasp.

"Ohh, I did not see that little twist comin'. What a way to keep you wantin' more."

"No kidding," he agrees. "Wanna start the next one?"

"Hell yes!"

Three episodes later, we're both yawning and falling asleep.

"I think it's time for bed," he says. "I still need to shower since Tyler's picking me up at seven tomorrow."

Shit, now I feel bad for keeping him up this late. "Sorry. I wouldn't have kept you up if I'd known."

He stands and stretches, giving me a nice sneak peek of his torso.

"Nah. I'll be fine. I consider it a luxury to binge-watch shows with you and be exhausted the next day. Haven't done that in ages."

I swallow hard, getting to my feet so I can clean the kitchen before I call it a night. Sassy's passed out, so I call for her, then take her out back.

Archer goes to the bathroom, and the water turns on. Picturing him in the shower is enough to make me double-check that my vibrator is charged.

Once Sassy's done outside, I rinse off the rest of the dishes. Sassy returns to the living room and waits for me to finish.

Just as I'm loading the dishwasher, Archer rounds the

corner. Water drips down his muscular shoulders and back, and I'm temporarily frozen in place as my eyes drop to the towel hanging low around his waist.

My fingers slip, and a plate falls to the floor, crashing loudly. Archer turns just as I quickly reach and pick it up.

"You okay?" he asks, walking over. "Did it break?"

"No, it's fine." I place it in the rack and try not to stare, but the scent of his clean skin is overpowering. "How was your shower?"

"Great. Well, I'm heading in, unless you'd like some help?" He cocks a brow, and as much as I'd *love* his company, there's no way I can be around him looking and smelling like this.

"Nah, go ahead. I'm almost done." I swallow hard, taking in his tattoo-covered chest. My gaze falls to the tattoos on his arms. "You'll have to tell me the meaning of those someday."

He looks down and frowns. "Maybe."

Since he doesn't want to talk about them right now, I drop it.

Sassy walks over and sniffs Archer's hand, then licks it. I hold back a laugh because we're thinking the same thing—he looks good enough to eat. Though if I'm not mistaken, Sassy's expression just said *I licked it, so he's mine.*

"Good night, Sassy." Archer pets her head, then smiles at me. "See ya in the morning."

"Night."

As soon as he's out of sight, I blow out a breath. I'm gonna need more than just my vibrator tonight.

Once the dishwasher's loaded and running, Sassy follows me into my room—though I'm surprised she didn't run after Archer by how she claimed him. I brush my teeth and do my skincare routine before climbing under the covers. I direct Sassy to the floor and bring out BUB—my backup boyfriend.

After removing my yoga pants, I dim the lights and turn on some soft music.

Usually, I look up some videos to get started, but Archer's given me plenty of visual inspiration to get me started.

Archer's hard chest.

Archer's broad back.

Archer's biceps and tattoos.

Archer's thighs in black jeans.

Archer's tongue when he licks his lips.

Archer's ass in a white cotton towel.

Archer's scruffy jawline and boyish face I want to sit on.

Archer's nipple ring that—

"Oh God…*yesyesyes*…" I whimper as softly as I can.

Reaching above my head, I push against the headboard and add more pressure to my clit. My calves tighten, tingles shoot up my spine, and my pussy clenches as the orgasm builds.

The explosion has my back arching as I chase the high. I can barely catch my breath when another begins to surface. I widen my legs and thrust my hips, seeking another release. The first one was intense, but this one is zapping me into outer space.

"*Holy shit…*" I nearly scream out but bite my lip to keep my voice from echoing. My back flies off the mattress as I seek a third orgasm.

"Yes, so close…" My eyes roll, my toes curl, and I'm seconds away…

Crash.

My body tumbles down as the wooden frame gives out, and my mattress falls to the floor.

What the fuck?

I turn off BUB, shocked as hell.

93

You've got to be kidding me!

As soon as I hear a knock on my door, I toss the vibrator and try to get up. Sassy barks like a lunatic at the noise, and I reassure her that everything's fine.

"Everleigh, you alright? I heard a bang."

"Yes, come in."

Without another word, he whips open the door and looks for me. His eyes drop to my legs, and I remember I'm still in a thin T-shirt and panties.

"What the hell?"

"Fuckin' IKEA bed, I swear."

"The boards busted?" He stands next to me, looking over the mess. Once I let Sassy inspect me, she saunters off to the living room.

"Yeah, I wood glued them together once."

He chuckles. "How many times has this happened?"

A blush covers my cheeks—he definitely knows how it busted, considering how I look.

"A few…" I reply. "It might be time for me to replace it if I can't fix it again."

"Well, let's lift the mattress and look at the damage," Archer suggests.

As soon as I move my comforter out of the way, BUB rolls out and thumps next to me. Archer's eyes widen in surprise.

"*Whoops.*" I chuckle, then kick it away.

We lift the mattress and lean it against the wall.

"Yep, just as I suspected." I frown at the slats that are cracked right next to where I repaired them before. "I don't have the shit to fix it. Go figure."

"Did you use clamps to hold them in place and wait for it to dry?"

"Uh, no."

His mouth tips up in amusement. "Might be time for some new slats."

Releasing a sigh, I nod. "I think you're right."

"I can go with you to the hardware store tomorrow and fix it for ya. Might take a couple of days, though."

"Okay, thanks. I guess I'll sleep on the couch tonight."

"Everleigh, no." Archer immediately comes closer. "Take my room. Please."

"Nah, I'll be fine. Won't be the first and probably not the last time I'll sleep there."

"There's no way I'm sleeping in my bed while you're on a lumpy couch."

"Hey!" I scold. "My couch isn't lumpy."

Archer smirks, and I know he's messing with me.

"Whatever. It's no biggie." I grab my pillow and comforter, but Archer blocks me from leaving.

"I hope you're going to the guest room with that." He crosses his arms, and it reminds me more of a big brother than a roommate.

"There is no guest room. That's yours," I say. "And honestly, I don't mind."

"So damn stubborn," he tsks, shaking his head, then quickly leans down. Before I realize what he's doing, he lifts me over his shoulder. His hands are on my bare thighs, and I'm suddenly aware of how close his face is to my panties.

"Excuse me!" I squeal as he walks through the living room. I release the items I was holding.

"Hey, caveman. I can walk!" I smack his ass as he steps into his room.

"I gave you the chance, and you didn't take it." He tosses me on the mattress and towers over me like a bodyguard.

"If you wanted me in your bed, Archer, all you had to do was ask," I taunt.

"Go to sleep. I'll be on the sofa."

Archer tries to leave, but I quickly stop him. "Wait!" He turns to face me with a frown. "I'm only staying in here if you are."

CHAPTER NINE

ARCHER

"WAIT!" she shouts eagerly.

I frown and spin around.

"I'm only staying in here if you are."

Everleigh stares at me with an intensity I've never felt before. She's not wearing any bottoms, and it's obvious she was using her vibrator. The thought of that nearly had me hard. Everleigh's the most beautiful woman I've ever met. She's not only gorgeous on the outside but her generosity and personality shine throughout. She let a complete stranger live with her and refuses to take anything in return beyond my friendship.

But this is where I draw the line, particularly when she's half-naked.

Her bluntness shouldn't surprise me anymore, especially after the past two weeks of being here, but right now, she's caught me off guard.

I should tell her no.

I should walk out and shut the door.

I should not be contemplating climbing under the covers with her.

Tyler would kill me, and if he doesn't, I'm pretty sure having Everleigh that close would.

"Well?" she taunts with an arched brow. "You stay with me, or I'm telling everyone you made me sleep on the couch. Oh, and I don't sleep with pants on."

I want to laugh because I've definitely noticed. I see right through this game she's playing, yet I want to take my turn.

Shrugging, I lower my joggers and stand in only my boxers. "Neither do I."

Watching Everleigh's eyes widen gives me a thrill. She hadn't expected me to strip down to my underwear and agree. I already wasn't wearing a shirt, and now we're both showing more skin than not.

Everleigh crawls off the bed and moves the sheets back before scooting beneath them. After I turn off the light, I slide in next to her.

"Stay on your side," I tell her teasingly.

"Yeah, sure." She snorts. Her toes press against my leg, and the feel of her touch makes me realize how big of a fucking mistake this is. "You're like a warm pillow."

I snicker. "And your feet are freezing."

She inches closer, wrapping her hands around my arm and squeezing while sliding her other foot under me. "Good thing I have my own personal heater."

Yep, I'm so fucking fucked.

It's silent for a few minutes until Everleigh speaks up. "So…you don't have to answer this, but what was it like for you and Annie growing up? From what you've told me, it sounds similar to Tyler's and my childhood."

Her soft and sincere voice makes me want to share

everything. Everleigh would probably understand more than most people and without judgment. Yet I can't tell her the tragic details, mostly because I've blocked them out.

Truthfully, it's embarrassing. Even though I couldn't control where we lived or our situation, when people hear about it, things become awkward. They pity me, I hate it, and the silent tension takes over. Plus, I don't want Everleigh to know that Annie and I went hungry for years. We never had new clothes. We stole to survive and denied it when asked. I instructed Annie to never tell an adult because if CPS showed up, they'd separate us. We needed each other, and I couldn't risk us being split apart and put into different foster homes. Regardless of our shitty home life, I still loved our mother. When she was sober and clean, at least.

"I don't have a lot of happy memories," I admit. "Annie's the only reason I stayed. Thought about running away dozens of times, but I couldn't leave her. Living on the streets was no problem for me, but she wouldn't have survived. Not without getting assaulted, at least. So I stayed to protect her. Our mom overdosed during Annie's senior year and never got to see her graduate."

That thought sends a fire of anger through me. Even though our mom was a hot mess on her best days, it was important to Annie. I barely got my diploma, but Annie and Mom were still there to cheer me on as I crossed the stage.

"I can tell you're the protective type. Annie's lucky to have a brother like you. Tyler basically raised me too, but after high school, he joined the military, and I moved in with our grandparents."

"Tyler told me about that. I'm glad you were in a safe place after he left."

She sighs briefly, her chest rising and falling. "I hate that she lives in the same town but never puts in any effort to see us. She hasn't met Scarlett, didn't send a wedding or baby gift to Tyler and Gemma, and doesn't check on me. It's almost worse that she's alive and chooses not to be involved. It'd probably hurt less if she was dead."

It's obvious how bothered she is by it. After I lost Mom, I didn't feel any void. She was hardly present, but I sympathize with wanting to have a parent in your life.

"What about your dad?" she asks.

"He left before Annie was born. I was only two. Don't know him, don't remember him."

"Guess we have a lot more in common than I thought." She tilts her head and looks over at me. With our faces almost touching, I could easily press my lips to hers.

"Is that why you have daddy issues?" I tease to lighten the mood.

"Yep. Same reason you probably have mommy issues," she throws back.

I chuckle because she's not wrong. I have a whole laundry list of issues.

"Oh, you have *no* idea."

"I know why you went to prison. You're not the brooding badass you try to portray," she states matter-of-factly.

"Considering you allowed a complete stranger—who's an ex-con—to move in with you, I figured you did. That or you're textbook crazy."

"That's definitely possible too. But even before I knew, it wouldn't have mattered. You're Tyler's friend, and he trusts you. That's all it took for me to know I wouldn't regret helping you. And so far…" She smiles. "I don't."

I blow out a breath of laughter. "Glad to hear that, I guess."

"If I'm being honest…once I heard you had tats and a

tragic past, I was sold." She flashes a cocky smirk, and I shake my head. "What's your type?"

My type? Blond hair, blue eyes, smart-mouthed and beautiful on the inside and out. One-hundred percent Everleigh.

"That sounds like a trick question I should avoid answering."

She snorts. "If I had to guess, it's someone who's stable, secure, and successful. The three S's."

"What makes you say that?" I ask, aware that also describes her.

"Isn't that what most men want to marry?"

"No idea. I've never been close to getting married."

"Me either. Farthest I've gotten is a third date, and that was years ago. Julien," she tells me in a French accent. "We met when I was twenty-five, and he was thirty-five. Flew me to Paris for our last date. I was so smitten and thought he was too. But then he asked me to move there for him."

"On the third date?" I nearly shout. Damn good thing I wasn't around then.

"Right! What kind of psycho maniac does that? That's how I knew he was not *the one*. Which was a bummer because he was loaded. Had a big package too."

I nearly choke on my tongue.

"You okay there?" she muses with a laugh.

"I'm starting to believe you enjoy catching me off guard."

"What you see is what you get with me. No bullshit, no fake personality, no pretending. It's a gift and a curse. Some people can't handle me."

I don't doubt that for a second. Hell, I hope *I* can survive her.

After a while, the room grows silent, and Everleigh's soft

snores tell me she's fallen asleep. She remains glued to my side, and I can't bear to pull away. I haven't had the comfort of sleeping next to someone like this in ages, and I want to soak it up.

It's just for tonight.

It means nothing.

We're just two friends—roommates—sharing a bed because hers broke.

No big deal.

My heart steadies, and as I'm finally drifting off, I hear Everleigh whisper. She must be a sleep talker. Then moments later, she nuzzles closer and moans my name.

"Archer."

I look at her, checking that she's asleep, and when she repeats herself a second later, my chest thuds harder.

Why the hell is she whimpering my name? More like *moaning*.

And why do I enjoy that thought so much?

She's dreaming of me. Or maybe she's fantasizing.

Either way, I cling to the thought. Against my better judgment, I snuggle into her and allow myself to touch her soft skin.

Then I drift off to sleep with the stupidest grin on my face.

"Archer."

My eyes flutter open and realize Everleigh is still pressed against me, except now her leg is hitched over my waist, and my cock has definitely noticed.

"Archer." I hear again and look over to Everleigh staring at me.

"Uh, hi. Good morning." I clear my throat.

"You're so warm and snuggly, like a big teddy bear. Hope you didn't mind me clinging to you," she says, gliding her fingers across my stomach.

"Nope. Barely noticed."

My dick decides at that moment to jerk, and my eyes widen in embarrassment. "Gotta use the bathroom, though."

"Oh, sorry. Yeah, me too. I should make some coffee and breakfast, then we can figure out how to fix my stupid bed." Everleigh pushes herself up, but instead of sliding off the mattress on the other side, she straddles my waist to get down.

"I can help with breakfast if you want," I say, covering my junk with my palms as she stands and stretches. Only wearing boxers was a bad fucking idea because I have more than just morning wood at the moment.

"Sure! I'll grind the beans, then change."

Everleigh finds Sassy at the door, waiting to go out. I watch her ass as she sashays away. Once she's out of view, I find some joggers and use the bathroom. I brush my teeth, then meet Everleigh in the kitchen. She's pouring two cups of coffee, then dumps a good amount of creamer in one.

"Here ya go." She gently slides mine across the breakfast bar with a smile.

"Thanks. Smells good."

"Tastes even better. I'm pretty serious about my coffee and wine."

Her tone makes me crack a smile. "So I've discovered."

"Do you think my bed is salvageable, or should I just skip the headache and buy another one?" she asks when I go to the fridge. I'm not a chef by any means, but I can whip up some cheesy scrambled eggs.

"I think we can make it work. If you have some tools, we can easily cut some wood to size."

"Hmm…well I don't, but Noah does. He's a professional fixer."

I snort at her choice of words. "I heard he helped with Katie's house. Is he a builder?"

"Kinda, but he fixes things too. Like a contractor. People hire him to do renovations but also fix random things around the house. A jack-of-all-trades, I guess you could say."

"Well…" I crack some eggs into a bowl while she continues to stare at my bare back as if I can't see her reflection in the microwave. "I might not have his skill level, but if you have a measuring tape, I'll get the size of your frame before we go."

"Oh, I do! Great idea. Then we can stop at Katie's on the way back if we need to."

"Sounds good."

I finish making breakfast and put some bread in the toaster.

Once they're done, I butter them and serve Everleigh.

"This looks awesome. You're becoming quite the little homemaker."

"I wouldn't say that."

"Oh come on, don't be offended. You can be a good cook and still be a manly man. I mean, you box all day long. You can't get much tougher than that." She takes a large bite of her eggs, then releases a loud moan. "Oh my God, so delicious. I'm keeping you forever."

I hold back a laugh. Everleigh talks nonstop, but I love it. There's never awkward silence when she's around and keeps things fun and interesting.

"Since you made the best breakfast ever, I'll load the dishwasher. Then we can go!" Everleigh jumps up. I tell her I'm going to change.

By the time I'm dressed and leave my room, Everleigh's on the couch petting Sassy. Though it's been an adjustment living with a dog, I've grown to like her a lot, and she's gotten used to me now. She's like her owner and disregards personal space. Sassy likes to jump on the furniture and sit right on me.

"The measuring tape is on the counter!" She points at it, and I grab it, then go to her room. After I've put the length and width into my phone, I go back to where she is.

"Ready?" she asks.

I give her a nod as she stands. "I texted Katie and gave her a heads-up that we might stop by. She said it was fine."

"Okay, great."

I follow Everleigh out the door and to her car. Ever since she mentioned seeing that black SUV around, I always look for it when I'm out. Luxury vehicles don't really exist in Lawton Ridge.

It only takes five minutes to drive to the hardware store.

When we walk in, I notice how universal these small-town shops are. The typical tools and necessities are here but also stacks of wood, lawn care equipment, work boots, a paint section, grills and fireplaces, and a random aisle of kitchen utensils. Honestly, it's kinda cool. Come for a gallon of paint, but leave with a new frying pan and a pair of shoes.

"Everleigh. How are ya?" a man finally comes from the back and greets us.

"Hey, Tim! I'm great. This is my roommate, Archer. Not sure if you've met him yet."

She introduces us, and he gives me a curious little look, but I ignore it.

Everleigh explains what happened and what she needs. He points out the lumber, wood glue, and clamps. As he's cutting the wood to our exact measurements, the front door chimes. Over the sounds of the saw, Tim shouts that he'll be right there. I glance over my shoulder and see a silhouette, but I don't get a good look before they disappear down another aisle.

Tim leads us around, and it feels like someone's watching us. Perhaps I'm paranoid, but my gut is hardly wrong.

While Tim rings up Everleigh's items, I stay guarded in place while looking around the store. I hear footsteps but don't see who they belong to.

"I'm leaving here in thirty minutes if you want me to come over and help."

My attention snaps to Tim.

What the hell?

I've literally been next to Everleigh this whole time, and he's been staring at her inappropriately. I assume everyone here is just neighborly, but there's something suggestive in his tone that's more sexual than friendly.

"I'm taking care of it," I respond before Everleigh can. "Since I'm the one who kinda broke it, I just figured I should be the one to fix it."

I stand with my arms crossed, staring the gawker down. He doesn't reply, just simply nods, then tells Everleigh her total.

"Thanks, Tim!" she calls out as we exit.

As we walk toward her car, I can feel her eyes burning a hole in the side of my face. "I know what you're going to say."

"Is that so?" she muses, pulling out her keys and unlocking the door. "Enlighten me."

I glance around, and my heart nearly stops when I see an Escalade parked across the street. That's when I notice someone in all black leaving the hardware store. I can't tell if it's a man or woman by the way the hood shields their face. I'm tempted to haul ass over there, but since I'm on parole, I need to be on my best behavior, which means not getting into fights or drawing attention to myself. If I'm being followed or if Chad's family is after me, I can't retaliate without reason.

Everleigh quickly moves her gaze to the black SUV as it speeds away.

"Did you see who it was?" she asks in a panic.

"No." I shake my head. "They were in the hardware store with us, though."

Everleigh's brows furrow, and I feel bad that I'm putting her in this position. She looks worried, and it's my fault she's living with fear. Staying here puts her and Tyler at risk. I should do the right thing and leave.

"If I had to guess, it's probably a friend or family member of a local resident who has a crush on you. Hopefully seeing me with you scared them off." She flashes me a wink, then gets behind the wheel.

Well then. Everleigh isn't fazed at all. Perhaps it's an act because she sounded concerned when she spotted the unusual vehicle before.

"Everleigh." I turn toward her when I buckle. "You and I both know it wasn't an admirer."

"Well, whoever it was is gone now." She shrugs, and her casualness throws me off. "Plus, we need to talk about your little caveman stunt back there."

Everleigh pulls out into the street, her words putting me on the spot.

"He was being rude," I say. "He was basically inviting himself over to your house."

"I could've defended myself," she states.

"He needed to be put in his place."

Everleigh snort-laughs, and it's the most adorable thing I've ever heard. "Is that so? Because I think you were the one trying to manifest your way into my bed."

"Considering you were in mine last night, it wouldn't take much to get into *yours*."

"Hey!" she snaps, taking a swing at me. "You callin' me easy?"

"Of course not! You're the one making it sexual. I was talking about sleeping."

She turns and glares at me. "Right."

I look away with a smirk.

Once we're back at the house, we immediately get to work. Once I replaced the broken panels, I glued and screwed them in, then clamped both sides.

"Need to let it cure for at least twenty-four hours before adding any weight," I tell her. "Then we can put the mattress back."

"So I guess I'll be your sleeping buddy for one more night," she muses.

The following evening, I check to make sure the slats are good and sturdy on the frame. Then we set the mattress on top, and she remakes her bed.

"Looks good as new," she says. "Wanna test it out?"

Everleigh waggles her brows, and I shake my head with a grin. Without a word, I scoop her up and toss her on it.

"*Oh my God!* A warning next time!" she scolds.

"Just wanted to make sure it wasn't gonna break on ya." I shrug teasingly.

"Maybe I should get out my vibrator and really test it out." Her seductive tone has the blood flowing right to my cock. The little evil minx.

"Are you blushing?" she taunts, scooting off to stand in front of me. "I think you are."

"I think you're enjoying this."

"I enjoy lots of things." The corner of her lips tilts up suggestively, and that's when I know I need to leave.

"I'm going to go to sleep now." I turn and walk toward the door. "Good night."

"Night, roomie."

I get under my covers and stare up at the ceiling. Each day it gets harder to be around Everleigh. Not because she's difficult to live with but because I find myself enjoying her company so much. She always makes me laugh, which feels good. I wish I could kiss those flirty, luscious lips, but I can't, and it's pure fucking torture. Doesn't help that Everleigh tempts me at every opportunity.

The sounds of my door creaking open and then her tiptoeing against the floor have me on high alert.

"What's wrong?" I immediately ask.

"I can't sleep," she says. "There's a draft in my room."

I arch a brow because I didn't feel one the several times I was in there.

"I think I sleep better next to you," she adds. "Would you mind if I crashed in here?"

As I lower my gaze down her body, I notice she's not wearing pants again. I'm in only my boxers, but I can't deny her, especially when I want to hear her whispering my name again.

"Sure, c'mon in," I say casually. "I see you're wearing socks this time."

"Figured you couldn't refuse me if I promised not to put my cold feet on you," she explains, crawling over my waist to get to the other side of the bed. "But since I didn't have to convince you, off they go!" She giggles, tossing them to the floor.

"You're horrible."

Wrapping my arm around her, I pull her close. She rests an arm over my chest and settles against me. If anyone walked in right now, they'd think we were a couple.

"In case you wondered, the bed held up against the vibrator."

I groan inwardly. "IKEA for the win," I force out.

She snickers. "I'll make sure to tell Tim…since he was so invested and all."

"Tim's a fucking creep."

"And he's like in his fifties. Small-town people offer their services without expecting *anything* in return," she informs me.

"Is Tim married?" I ask.

She thinks for a moment. "No."

"Does Tim have a dick?" I continue.

She chuckles. "I assume he does."

"Then he wasn't offering to be nice. He was staring at you like he wanted to eat you for breakfast. Trust me, Tim wanted something in return."

"You must've been observing him quite intensely then."

"It wasn't hard to notice, Everleigh. You need to be more careful. Guys see you, and they'll take whatever the hell they want, whether you're willing or not," I tell her sternly, my arm tensing.

Everleigh glances at me, but I don't look at her. My lips are in a tight line as I imagine what I'd do to any guy who hurt her.

"Archer, you don't have to worry about me so much. I'm pretty tough, even for my size," she says with a little chuckle. "I've had to look out for myself for years."

"Well you shouldn't have to and won't now that I'm here."

Everleigh places a palm over my cheek, and the heat of her skin sends intense waves of electricity down my body. "You're a good guy, Archer. I hope someday you'll let me look out for you too."

CHAPTER TEN

EVERLEIGH

I DANCE around the kitchen as I listen to Christmas tunes. I bellow out the chorus of Mariah Carey's "All I Want for Christmas."

Sassy gives me a judgy stare, but I don't care. Mariah has *nothing* on me.

Not only is it Christmas Eve and the happiest time of the year but the past two and a half weeks have also been the absolute best. The boutique has been busier than ever. The new men's line has sold out twice since I debuted it, and I already have pre-orders for my March clothing launch.

Though I've always loved the holidays, having Archer here has made it even more special. He's frosted cookies and shopped in Mobile with me, and has allowed me to sleep in his bed every night since that first time.

I truly don't think I realized how lonely I was until he arrived. I've always been a social person and even liked living alone, but Archer's presence gives me something to look forward to.

While our sleeping arrangement is unconventional, neither

of us has brought up the conversation of stopping. What's even weirder is that I've never slept with a man without having sex. The only point of getting into a man's bed was to get off, and though I'm tempted to tear off Archer's clothes nearly every minute of the day, I've controlled myself. We've developed this bond, a friendship that's already unbreakable, and he makes me feel safe. We're like an old married couple—we watch specific shows with each other, take turns cooking, and drink our morning coffee together. And though I wish we could be more, spending time and being friends with him is enough.

Okay, scratch that.

I want him to rip off my panties with his teeth.

I want to suck on his nipple ring, and I want to watch him unravel as I ride him.

And by the way his body responds to mine, I'm positive he wants the same.

Neither of us is willing to make a move, mainly because of my overbearing brother and his stupid rule. Archer's loyal to him, and I don't want to be the reason he breaks that. But I swear to God, I might die from the tension between us.

"That's some very *off-pitch* singing," Archer teases as he walks out of the bathroom just wearing a towel. Though I've seen him half-naked a dozen times now, it never gets old.

"You kissed your gram with that mouth?" I tsk. "That's not very gentlemanly."

The edges of his lips tilt up into a cocky smirk. "Never said I was."

I rest a hand on my hip. "If you're gonna fit in with the Southerners, you better learn some manners."

Archer's chuckle radiates heat between my thighs. "My apologies, queen. May I bow down and kiss your royal feet?"

"Do it, and I'll knee you where the sun doesn't shine," I retort.

"My ankles? How rude."

I snort, shaking my head. "Hurry up and get dressed so you can help me decorate the gingerbread cookies."

"Yes, ma'am."

"There's that Southern accent," I tease. "You'll be saying *y'all* and *howdy* in no time."

"God, I hope not," he mumbles, walking to his room.

While I wait for Archer, I gather up the gifts from under the tree and put them in a box. Tonight is our friends' gift exchange at Noah and Katie's house, and I have volunteered to bring the sweets. Of course, I spoil my nieces and nephews rotten with loads of presents. Archer and I have agreed to exchange gifts tomorrow morning, but I'm bringing one for him to open tonight.

"Wow, you clean up very nicely," I say when he returns. Dark jeans sit perfectly on his hips, and he's tucked in a dark button-up shirt that's rolled to his elbows. Those damn tats taunt me every time he shows them off.

"Figured I had to up my game since you're all dressed up." His eyes wander down to my legs, then back up to my chest, admiring my dress along the way.

"Well, of course I did." I smirk. "Okay, add some candy buttons, and I'll do the sprinkles."

"I see you left the dicks off this time," he muses.

"There will be children around," I remind him.

We get the rest of the cookies decorated, then he helps load the car. Though I haven't spotted the black SUV since it sped off outside the hardware store, I still keep an eye out for it because I'm not convinced it was just a tourist. After Gemma brought up the idea that I could be a person of interest in

Eric's murder, I've been more paranoid that someone's watching me.

"Aunt Everleigh! Uncle Archer!" Owen calls out, then rushes to give me a hug. I absolutely adore that he already considers Archer family because we are, regardless of blood.

"Hey, buddy! Merry Christmas!" I kiss the top of his head. "I swear, you've grown an inch since Thanksgiving."

Archer gives him a fist bump. "Yeah, he'll be taller than me soon."

Owen grins. "I'm almost taller than Mom," he informs us.

"That's not hard to accomplish," I tease when Katie comes into view. "Probably taller than Gemma already."

"I heard that," she calls from somewhere in the house.

Archer carries the gifts into the living room as I bring the tray of cookies into the kitchen.

"Hey, sis." Tyler gives me a side hug.

"Hello…Merry Christmas, y'all!" I go around, hugging everyone.

"Where are Jerry and Belinda?" I ask.

We go into the living room, where Archer and Owen are chatting about boxing.

"They're off celebrating," Gemma answers. "Dad *finally* popped the question."

"What? No way!" I exclaim. "That's so exciting."

"Speaking of…" Katie interjects. "We set a date for next summer in Magnolia Springs."

"About time!" I wrap my arm around her. "That time of year will be stunning."

"Where's that?" Archer asks.

"It's just over an hour away," Noah explains. Archer and I sit next to each other on the couch, though we're not close enough to touch.

"It's this quaint little town that my grandmother used to live in, and we'd go visit every summer. One time, Noah came with me, and last April, he surprised me with a weekend trip to a B&B. Ever since, we knew we wanted to get married there." Katie beams at Noah, who's holding one of the twins.

"I can't wait," I say. "We better get to planning."

"Small and simple," Katie says, giving me a warning glare. "I'm aware of how extra you get."

"Uh," I gasp. "I may never get married, and my brother went and got hitched without telling anyone, so yours might be the only one I'll ever help plan."

"You can plan mine, Aunt Everleigh," Owen informs me.

"Aw…thanks, bud. You have a bride in mind already?" I ask in a teasing voice. "Because if so, we only have seven years until you're eighteen. I better start now."

Owen rolls his eyes as he rocks the other twin baby.

"You tryin' to give me a heart attack?" Katie scolds.

Her panicked tone has me chuckling.

"I hope someone warned you, Archer," Gemma says to him. "You stay with Everleigh long enough, she might trick you into walking down the aisle with her."

"I wouldn't have to *trick* him, thank you very much." I shoot her a glare. "He's already offered to kiss my feet and make me his queen."

A round of laughter echoes from everyone except my unamused brother, who's glancing between Archer and me. But we're not even touching, so I don't know what his problem is.

"Relax, Tyler. Geez," I tease.

"Blink twice if you need help," he directs to Archer.

I grab a throw pillow from the couch and chuck it at Tyler.

"Can we open presents now?" Owen asks, thankfully redirecting the conversation away from me.

"After we get the food in the oven," Katie tells him as Gemma and I move to the kitchen to help. "Then we will while they're baking."

It's been our tradition to get together for years. We have homemade pizza, snacks, and desserts, then exchange presents. After that, we watch a Christmas movie. Since Katie and Gemma are breastfeeding, we opted out of having any alcohol this year.

"So Archer, now that you've been here for a month, how are you settlin' in?" Gemma asks. I add sauce to one of the pizzas, and Archer comes and puts pepperonis and mushrooms on another.

"Better than I thought I would, honestly. Feels like I've been here much longer. So far, everyone I've met has been friendly. I love working at the gym, and Everleigh's been a great roommate." He looks at me with a boyish grin. "I'm glad Tyler urged me to move here."

"Probably the second-best idea he's *ever* had," I muse. "Marrying Gemma being the first, of course."

Gemma snickers as Tyler flashes me a scowl.

"I ran into MaryAnn at the grocery store the other day. She said she loves her boxing lessons with you and that you have a waiting list now," Katie tells Archer. "You must be in high demand."

A wave of jealousy flutters through me because she's one of my customers who kept asking about him. After explaining several times that I wasn't running a single's club, she told me I was rude. Of course it wasn't hard to find him in this small town, and she quickly signed up to train with him.

"He is," Tyler confirms. "I had to put up a sign about not recording private lessons. People were posting them online."

Rage consumes me, and I'm tempted to tell Tyler to control his horny customers, but it'd do no good. I'd give myself away in front of everyone.

"MaryAnn said you two planned a date after New Year's," Katie adds. I keep my head down and focus on adding cheese and pineapple to mine.

Archer clears his throat, and his eyes burn a hole into the side of my face. "Well, *no*. She asked if I wanted to go out for a drink sometime, and I told her I was really busy at the moment, which I am, and that maybe I'd have more free time after the new year."

"I worked on her house a couple of months ago," Noah says, oblivious to the thick tension in the air. "She's really nice."

Archer nods in agreement, and I wonder if he wants to go out with her. He's said he wasn't looking to date right now, but that could've changed. Perhaps I'm holding him back and keeping him captive in this *roommates who sleep in the same bed but can't touch* hell. It's obvious we have something brewing between us, but we've silently agreed not to cross that line. It's a constant battle to fight the attraction. All night long, our bodies press against each other, and though it's torturous, I look forward to it.

Now I'm wondering if it's a bad idea to get attached to him and vice versa. Especially if he does want to start dating.

Once the pizzas are in the oven, we bring the snacks into the living room and wait for them to cook. Owen opens his presents from me, Tyler, and Gemma. Archer surprised him with three sessions of boxing lessons with his parents' permission. Then he opened the twin babies' gifts and held them up for them to see. Of course they couldn't care less, but we watched in excitement anyway.

We pause to get the food out of the oven and sit back down in the living room to eat.

"Who the hell put pineapple on this?" Noah shouts, and I release a giggle.

"That one's mine!"

"A whole pie, woman? You better eat every bite," he warns in his dad voice.

"I love pineapple on pizza," Archer interjects. "I can help you with it."

"You do? Why didn't I know that?" I give him a look, then realize we've never actually made pizza together. "We're gonna have to start having pizza nights now. It's a rarity to find someone who actually eats pineapple like me."

"Sounds like a match made in heaven," Gemma sing-songs.

Tyler arches his brow at her, and she quickly adds, "For roommates, I mean."

I roll my eyes at her pathetic save. Tyler's not gonna let this go. What a vagina killer.

Once we've all eaten our weight in pizza and snacks, we continue the gift exchange. I place a small box in Archer's lap. "For you."

"I thought we were waiting until tomorrow?" He eyes it curiously.

"Oh we are, but I wanted you to open this one early." I smile.

Archer rips off the paper and lifts the top. "A watch?"

"An Apple watch," I explain. "I figured since you work out and train so much, you'd like to record your stats. It tracks a ton of other stuff too, plus you can get phone calls and text messages if you don't have your phone on you. It's pretty cool."

Archer looks at me like he's torn on how to react. I kinda figured he'd say he couldn't accept it, so I came prepared.

"Before you tell me it's too much, I want you to have it." I hold up my wrist to show him mine. "Now we can challenge each other with exercise competitions. It could be fun."

Archer's eyes soften as he flashes me a tender smile. "Wow. Thank you. You'll have to teach me how to use it."

"I think you might be the only one who can beat her," Katie says. "She always wins because she walks five miles a day around the boutique."

"Yeah, she *cheats*. Especially since I'm on maternity leave," Gemma adds with a scowl.

"I'm not cheating! You're the ones who accept the challenge," I remind them.

"Because if we don't, you call us big losers." Katie snickers.

I roll my eyes at their dramatics. "Don't believe them," I tell Archer. "But she's right. You'll probably kick my butt. Maybe not, though. I'm *super* competitive."

Archer chuckles. "Looking forward to it."

We spend the rest of the evening watching *National Lampoon's Christmas Vacation*. I lean against Archer as he sits next to me on the floor. The warmth of his body reminds me why I love sleeping next to him, but I think it's time I go back to my room. Regardless of how addicted I am to him.

"Love you guys." I give Katie and Gemma a hug. The babies went to bed hours ago, but I sneak a kiss on Scarlett's cheek before Tyler puts her in the car seat.

"See you tomorrow, brother," I say, waving to everyone as Archer says his goodbyes. We always go to our grandparents' house on Christmas Day, and of course, I'm dragging my roommate with me.

"I'm so ready to sleep," I say once we make it home.

"Wait. Since I opened one of your gifts early, I want to give you one of mine," Archer tells me before I can escape to my room.

"Are you sure? I can do it tomorrow."

"Fair is fair," he taunts.

"Fine." I smile.

Archer hands me a bag. "Not much of a wrapper, sorry."

I grin as I pull out the tissue paper. "Oh my gosh, Archer." I bark out a laugh when I hold up the T-shirt. It reads, *Don't mess with me* on the front, and then, *I'm blond, Southern, and my roommate will kick your ass* on the back. "This is hilarious."

"Hope you like it."

"I love it." I close the space between us and wrap my arms around him. "Thank you." I release him, then hold the shirt to my chest. "I'm gonna wear it to bed."

After I take out Sassy and turn off the lights, I go to my room. I put on the T-shirt and crawl under my covers. Sassy joins me at the foot of the bed, and I immediately feel the loss of not having Archer next to me.

Though I'm exhausted, I can't seem to fall asleep. I keep thinking about Archer and if he's waiting for me or if he's relieved to finally have the bed to himself. If I didn't love my brother or understand how important it is to Archer not to disappoint him, I would've already crossed the line.

Just as I start to drift off, I hear loud footsteps, and then my door swings open. My eyes widen at my bare-chested roommate, and without a word, he marches in and tears off the covers.

"What the hell are you doing?" I squeal when he lifts and

carries me over his shoulder. "Archer!" I can't stop my laughter as he walks out.

"Apparently, I can't fall asleep without you in my bed, hogging my blankets, putting your cold feet on me, and moaning my name. It's like a drug. I need it," he admits, then tosses me on top of his mattress. I had no idea I was saying his name in my sleep, but I'm not really surprised, considering how much the thought of him consumes me.

"I was worried being in here was torture for you," I admit softly. "I've noticed the way your body reacts to mine and didn't want to be the reason you don't go on dates."

The vulnerability in my tone isn't something I'm used to. However, when it comes to Archer, I want to show him all sides of me, even if he's not ready to share all of his with me.

With a tight and serious expression, he towers over me with his hands on either side of me.

"Fuck, Everleigh, it is. Every goddamn night, I fight not to touch you. I struggle to keep my fingers out of your little cotton panties, but I'd rather set myself on fire than not have you in here with me. Consider me co-dependent."

His face is so close to mine, it'd only take an inch or two to press my mouth to his.

But considering how hard this is for both of us, I don't move.

Swallowing, I nod. "I'm not going anywhere, Archer. I'll sleep in here for as long as you allow me to."

When he leans down, I close my eyes, and his lips gently press on my forehead. Our first kiss wasn't where I needed his touch the most, but I'll take anything he's willing to give me— even if it kills me in the end.

CHAPTER ELEVEN

ARCHER

I WAKE up to the smells and sounds of frying bacon. Rolling over, I grab my cell phone and check the time—almost seven. Deciding to get up, I look at the Santa pajamas left for me on Everleigh's side of the bed. The note on top says *wear these*! She drew a heart and signed an E beside it. A smile touches my lips when I put them on.

Last night, there was no way in hell I was letting her sleep in her room, not when I needed her close—regardless of how hard it is for me. I can't believe I've already been here a month, and I am already fighting against falling for her. She hasn't exactly made it easy for me, and she's buried herself deep inside my thoughts.

Once I'm dressed, I find Everleigh in the kitchen. She's standing at the stove wearing the shirt I got her and some shorts. If you want to call them that since they barely cover her ass. Of course, there are miniature reindeer on them. While she's occupied, I take my time drinking in every inch of her. Eventually, she turns and notices me, and a grin slides across her lips.

"Good mornin'! I'm makin' us breakfast." She studies my tattoos.

I move and stand beside her, seeing Sassy begging at her feet. I look at the ingredients on the counter, plus the food she's already cooked. "Bacon, eggs, hash browns, and pancakes?"

"Of course, Christmas morning tradition! Also, I've got red and green syrup and whipped cream." She bumps me with her hip, then notices what I'm wearing. "You look good in those."

"Everleigh, you didn't have to get me anything else. Seriously, that Apple watch is amazing." I lift my wrist, showing her that I have it on. She's so goddamn generous, and I wish I could spoil her too.

"Excuse me? Yes, I did. I love buying things for the people in my life. Also, I made some coffee." She takes the bacon out of the skillet, then starts whipping up the pancakes.

"You've already done more than enough."

Her face softens. "And I'm gonna keep doing more."

"I'll never be able to repay you if you keep gifting me things and doing so much for me," I say. I hate owing her because I grew up doing what I could for my sister and me. Always doing things on your own and not expecting anything in return is a hard habit to break.

"You don't owe me anything, Archer. I do things because I like to, not because I expect anything in return. It makes me happy to make the people I care about happy." Everleigh has no idea how much her words make my body ignite. I care about her so damn much already.

"You're amazing, you know that?" I fill a mug full of her strong-ass coffee.

"I try." She smirks.

Once our pancakes have a whipped cream beard like Santa,

Everleigh leads me to the living room. Sassy follows in our wake, finds her place on the floor, and stares as we eat.

"This is another one of my annual traditions," she explains around a mouthful, pointing at the Christmas special on TV. "Next up, we're opening presents."

I look over at the tree and notice all the boxes stuffed under it.

"I've never had a Christmas quite like this," I admit with an appreciative grin.

"There'll be many more. Don't you worry."

Just as the show we're watching ends, our plates are cleared, and I put them in the sink. My watch buzzes, and I see it's my sister on FaceTime, so I quickly grab my phone.

As soon as I answer, Annie smiles at me.

"Merry Christmas, sis," I tell her.

"You too! Whatcha doing?" Behind her, Sadie's on the floor surrounded by colorful wrapping paper.

"Just finished breakfast and watching TV. What time did you wake up?" I laugh, seeing the bags under her eyes. She moves the phone closer to her lips and whispers, "Four. In. The. Fucking. Morning."

I scrunch my nose. "Nooooo, thank you."

"No kidding. Way too damn early."

"Oh, there's someone I want you to meet," I say before Everleigh can run off.

She pops her head up with wide eyes, but I can tell she's excited to finally be formally introduced. The last time we talked, Sadie bombarded Everleigh with questions before she walked away.

Everleigh slides in beside me, smiling wide.

"This is my roommate, Everleigh. She owns a shop in town that has the shirts you like."

"Hi, Merry Christmas! It's so nice to finally meet you," Everleigh eagerly says.

"Same! I'm sure my brother has been boring, quiet, and has kept to himself the entire time there," she states.

I give her a stern look, and Everleigh laughs.

"Just a little. Still trying to crack that hard shell of his, but I'll get there." She wraps her arm around me, and just her simple touch drives me crazy.

"*Trust me*," she adds, giving me a smoldering look before pinching my side. I wiggle away from her.

"Oh, so you're ticklish? *Very* good to know..."

"See what you did." I glower at my sister as Everleigh chases me around the living room, using her fingers as pinchers.

Annie gets a kick out of it and cheers Everleigh on.

"Whose side are you on anyway?" I ask, trying to catch my breath as I put the couch between us.

"Okay, okay. I'll call a truce...for *now*." Everleigh comes back into view of our FaceTime call.

"Any other secrets you'd like to share about Archer?" She waggles her brows.

"Oh, the things I could say." Annie shakes her head. "But he might disown me if I spilled *all* the tea."

"Lose a brother, gain a sister. I think I'm a fair trade," Everleigh taunts, causing Annie to snort.

I playfully roll my eyes but adore how much Annie seems to already like Everleigh. "But anyway. I will give you two some privacy. I need to jump in the shower and start getting dressed for the day. It really was nice meeting you."

"So nice meeting you too. I'm gonna have Archer send me the links to your shop."

"Oh, please do. If there's anything you like, just let me

know, and I'll give you the family discount. Or you know…" Everleigh looks at me, then back at Annie. "You could always come visit?"

"Maybe one day!" Annie grins, and they wave goodbye.

Everleigh winks, then walks toward her room. Before she opens the door, she turns and looks at me with pure fire in her eyes. Things wouldn't be like this if we were two different people.

When I hear the water turn on, I plop down on the couch. Sassy jumps next to me and lays her head on my lap.

"I really like her," Annie offers. "She's adorable and seems like a lot of fun."

"Yeah, she is." I grin, wishing there was a chance in hell for us but knowing that there's not. "You two would get along great if you lived here. You'd probably be best friends."

Annie doesn't respond about moving, though I wonder if she's happy there. If she'd ever consider starting over in a new place. She's had a tough life, and I want to help change that and make it easier for her.

I see my niece walking toward her bedroom with toys in her hands, and she stops and hogs the screen. "Hey, Uncle Archer! Look what Santa brought me!"

"Is that an iPad?" I ask.

"Yes!" she squeals. "I put it on my list!"

"Santa splurged this year," Annie admits.

Ready to play with her new toy, Sadie speaks up. "Mom, can I go play now?"

"Sure, sweetie."

"Yay! Bye, Uncle Archer!"

Now that Sadie's gone, I know the questions are going to start since little ears are no longer in the room.

"You bought a five-year-old an iPad?" I whisper-laugh.

"Kids are smart these days! Trust me, she can use my cell phone better than I can."

"I can see I've missed a lot over the years."

She gives me a small smile and nods. A few silent seconds pass, and Annie speaks up. "So...you two hooking up?"

"What? No."

Doesn't mean I haven't thought about it more than I care to admit.

She narrows her eyes. "Why not? I could feel the sexual tension all the way in Wyoming. She's gorgeous, and I see the way you two look at each other."

I release a steady breath. "It's complicated. She's off-limits."

"Is she wearing a chastity belt or something?"

I shake my head.

"She's dating someone else?"

"No. Tyler's very protective of his sister and has made it crystal clear to both of us that he doesn't approve."

"What? Because of your past?" she asks, confused.

"No, nothing like that. He thinks I need time to restart my life before rushing into a relationship, and Everleigh's not the settling down type. He doesn't want either of us to get hurt or make it complicated since we're roommates. I'm just as protective as you, sis, so I can't fault him for it."

Sadness flashes in her eyes, and I know she's thinking about that night all those years ago. After sucking in a deep breath, she speaks up. "Yeah, I can see where he's coming from, but you're old enough to make your own decisions. If you believe you're ready for a relationship, then that's all that should matter. Perhaps if you told him how you felt, he'd be fine with it and—"

Immediately, I shake my head. "No. It's a terrible idea. He's done way too much for me, and I don't want there to be any bad blood between us. He trusts me, and I don't want to give him a reason not to. I have a really good thing going, and I don't want to mess up this opportunity to start fresh, ya know?"

"I suppose." She doesn't sound convinced.

I think about how much Tyler talked about Everleigh in prison. He loves her and just wants her to have the very best. Can't say I disagree because I'm certain she could do a hell of a lot better than me.

"So, I thought I saw Krystal in the grocery store the other day," Annie tells me, lowering her voice to a near whisper.

My brows furrow. "Chad's sister, Krystal?"

"Yeah, I thought it was strange too. Why would she be here of all places?"

Thoughts race through my mind as I try to understand why she'd be in Wyoming, considering Chad's family lives in Vegas.

"Are you positive it was her?"

Annie sighs, chewing on her bottom lip. "No, but it looked like her. Before I could confront her, she turned down an aisle, and too many people were in my way. I mean, it probably wasn't her, but I thought I'd mention it because it's making me anxious. She knows that restraining order means she's not supposed to be anywhere near me."

"I know. Keep an eye out," I demand.

"Anything weird been happening to you?"

Not wanting to worry her even more, I keep the sightings of the Escalade I think is following me to myself. "Not really. Please stay safe. If at any point you notice anything else, call the police. Get it documented right away."

"I'm on high alert, but it may just be my paranoia since the anniversary of..." She forces a smile. "You know how I get around the holidays. It could also be an overload of stress too," she admits.

"You need sleep. You look exhausted." She's been working longer shifts at the hospital since Thanksgiving.

"I know, I know. But Santa came, and school is out, so no rest for the wicked. Anyway, I should probably go make sure she isn't buying the entire app store right now because I haven't figured out how to turn it off yet. Sadie can probably figure it out before I can," she says with an amused laugh. "Don't be a stranger. Text or call me if you're lonely."

A smirk hits my lips. "Sure thing. Merry Christmas. I love you guys."

"We love you too," she says, and we end the call.

After setting my phone down, I get up and clean the kitchen. Since Everleigh cooked, it's the least I could do—something that's become our little tradition. If she cooks, I clean up, and vice versa.

As soon as I move to the plate of extra bacon, Sassy's at my feet. "You can have one if you keep it a secret," I whisper.

She does this spin-around trick Everleigh taught her, and I cave. She gobbles it up quickly, not leaving a trace behind.

A minute later, Everleigh walks into the kitchen with wet hair. She has on some different clothes, but I'm sure she'll change again before we head to her grandparents' this evening. "You're already finished chattin'?"

"Yeah, Annie had to go do mom stuff," I say over my shoulder as she moves into the living room, towel drying her hair.

"She's awesome. I was serious about her coming to visit sometime. Maybe we can capture her and make her move here too?"

I snort-laugh. "She'd love Lawton Ridge, but I dunno about the living here part. I think that'd take some bribing since she's settled in Wyoming and has a stable job at the hospital."

"Oh, she's a nurse?" Everleigh asks.

"Yep. She is, and a damn good one at that. She got her CNA before Scarlett was born and worked part-time through nursing school while being a single mom."

"Wow, your sister is a badass," Everleigh states, genuinely impressed.

A smile meets my lips. "She really is." For more reasons than one.

"Well, I'm convinced that if she came here, she'd never want to leave. It's an amazing town to raise kids. Also, I've heard the school nurse could be retiring soon."

From the kitchen, I tilt my head at her. "Seriously?"

"Yep, so who knows what could happen if she moved here." She looks at the shiny wrapping paper and grins. "Are you ready to open presents now?"

"Of course," I say, wiping my hands on a dish towel. We sit on the floor in front of the tree, and I feel like a kid again. Everleigh hands me one and then opens one herself.

I chuckle. "You bought yourself gifts?"

"Yep! The hard part was waiting until today. I buy myself little gifts all year long, then I wrap them up and keep them in my closet. The night before Christmas, I put them under the tree and try to remember what the hell I bought." She shakes the box as I rip off the snowflake paper from my bag.

I reach my hand inside and pull out a baseball cap. "Oh wow. I love this." I shake it out a bit and put it on my head.

"I noticed you didn't have one and most guys like to wear them, so I figured you needed one."

"Well, thank you. It's great."

131

"And it looks sexy as hell on you." She waggles her brows, then holds up a necklace. "I totally forgot about this!"

The way she surprises herself makes me laugh, but also, it's so like her. Everleigh makes no apologies for enjoying herself.

We exchange a few more gifts. She gushes over the fuzzy socks I got her. Then she opens the snarky coffee mug and six-month wine club subscription, which she claims it'll be for the both of us to drink during our TV shows.

"Wow, you know me so well, Archer." She looks at the things I bought her, then flashes me a grateful smile. "I love it all so much, thank you."

"You're welcome."

She hands me another box, and inside is a framed photo of Sassy. The next has a winter coat because apparently mine didn't look warm. After all the gifts under the tree are unwrapped, and the living room is a mess, I stand.

"Hold on. I have one more thing for you," I tell her.

She places her hand over her heart as she stays sitting. "Archer, you've given me enough."

"Yeah, but I love seeing you surprised," I say, then go to my room and grab it.

Everleigh's gaze meets mine when I hand it to her and kneel next to her. "Thank you. Whatever it is, I'm sure it's perfect."

"I hope so." And that she doesn't think it's a stupid idea.

She carefully unwraps the paper and pulls out a Polaroid camera. At first, she gasps, then squeals as she wraps her free arm around my neck. I allow her to sink into me as my hand snakes around her waist. My heart races, and I force myself to let go before I lower my head and crash my lips to hers.

Everleigh creates a little space, and I wonder if she felt the spark too. I do anytime we're close.

Clearing her throat, she speaks up. "Thank you, Archer. Thank you so much. I've been meaning to get one of these!"

"I was scared it'd be stupid, but you're so good at taking photos, and I thought—"

She closes the space between us and hesitates, "It's an amazing gift."

For a moment, I think she's going to give in to what we both want. I've never had the urge to kiss her more than I do right now. The room grows still, and right before *I* drum up the courage to make a move, her cell phone rings in her back pocket. I swear I hear her whisper a curse.

Clarity surrounds me, and I blow out a breath.

Everleigh answers, smiling wide with strawberry-colored cheeks. "Merry Christmas!"

She's flustered, and I get satisfaction seeing her like this. Our eyes lock together as she continues talking. "Yes, I'll be there. Archer too."

I know it's Tyler by how she's acting. It's the reality check I needed

"I'll tell him," she says, then hangs up.

"Tyler said Merry Christmas and he'll see you tonight at our grandparents' house."

My body stiffens, and she notices.

Before she can ask, I speak up. "I'm actually a little nervous to meet them. I never know what to expect."

"Oh, they're harmless. Mimi might try to kidnap you, though. Wouldn't be surprised if she offered you one of her spare rooms, but that's just how she is. Loves to do things for others. Unlike those other cougars in town who want to *actually* capture you."

I chuckle at the hint of jealousy in her tone. "She sounds wonderful. Must be where you get your generosity from."

"Yeah, she's great. She's actually less strict on me than my brother," Everleigh admits with a laugh, but I don't think she's joking. We clean up the living room, then Everleigh takes the camera from the box and calls for Sassy.

"Kneel beside her," she directs, bringing the viewfinder to one eye and squinting the other. I make sure to smile as Sassy leans over to lick me. Seconds later, Everleigh pulls it out and shakes it until the picture develops.

"Look at you two." She flips it around, smiling.

The way Sassy's staring at me is adorable. "That's great."

"My turn," she says, and I hold out my hand so she can get a pic with Sassy too.

"No, one with *you*!" She holds it up and somehow manages to take a selfie. Once our image appears, I see she's making kissy lips toward me.

"You're cute," I tell her, and she reaches over to try to tickle me, but I'm too fast. "Don't start that again."

Sassy starts barking and chases Everleigh around the living room with her tail wagging. She has the zoomies as she slides down the hall and then runs back toward Everleigh.

"Okay, okay! That's enough!" Everleigh breathlessly says. "Wasn't tryin' to get you worked up but thank you for the steps." She looks at her watch, then at me with an evil grin.

I cross my arms over my chest. "Don't prove your friends right. Challenge cheater."

She bellows out an evil laugh, which causes me to join her. Everleigh's happiness is contagious because I've never laughed this much before.

"Christmas movie time!" she announces, hopping on the couch and flicking on the TV. "Have to enjoy the last little bit of my favorite holiday while I can."

I sit next to her, and though we're only inches apart, our

gazes are glued to the screen. After a while, we get ready for dinner.

"Ready?" she asks an hour later. Her hair is in big curls, and she's wearing a dark green dress with red heels.

"Wow," I whisper, and she smirks.

"I'm gonna miss Christmas when it's gone." She sticks out her bottom lip, which I find so damn adorable.

"But we have New Year's," I remind her, and her excitement returns.

"Yes, you're right!" She looks me up and down. "Mimi isn't gonna let you leave, especially if you're wearing this tie."

Everleigh tugs on it, and my cock springs to life. If she's this fiery outside the bedroom, I can only imagine how she'd be between the sheets. Probably more than I could handle if I'm being honest. Before we leave, she takes Sassy out one last time.

On the way over, Everleigh talks about the shop, and I chat about the gym. Though neither of us mentions it, we're undoubtedly scanning the streets looking for the SUV. Within ten minutes, we're pulling up to a house that looks like it fell out of a Hallmark Christmas movie. The bushes are perfectly trimmed with colorful Christmas lights, and festive garland hangs from the porch.

As we walk on the sidewalk together, Everleigh loops her arm around mine, giving me all the confidence I need. She doesn't knock, and I follow her as she heads right in. The hearty smells of roasting turkey and sweet bread waft through the air, and it makes my stomach growl. We enter the kitchen, where an older man and woman sit at the breakfast nook drinking coffee.

"Howdy!" her grandfather says as Everleigh gives him a

side hug. Once they pull away, he stands and offers me his hand.

"This is Pops," Everleigh introduces.

"Nice to meet you," I say, shaking it in return.

"Pleasure's mine," he tells me with a big toothy grin.

Everleigh's grandma pulls me into a tight hug before I get the chance to say hello. "You can just call me Mimi. Happy to meet you, Archer. Hope you're hungry."

"Thank you. Starving," I say.

"Me too," a deep voice echoes from behind us.

Tyler laughs, and Gemma enters carrying Scarlett. We exchange greetings, and soon, Mimi steals Scarlett and rushes us to the dinner table. Plates are set out with dishes full of food. Casseroles, different potatoes, and veggies are passed around while Everleigh's grandfather carves the turkey. Before we eat, Pops says the blessing, and then we dig in.

"Everything's delicious," I say, meeting Mimi's eyes. "Best meal I've ever had."

"Thank you, sweetie," she beams.

After we're stuffed to the brim, Mimi insists we each eat a slice of her peach pie with a scoop of homemade vanilla ice cream.

"You can't say no," Everleigh whispers with a giggle. "It's *her* tradition."

"Considering I know how you are with yours, I'll gladly participate," I reply.

I feel Tyler studying us, but he doesn't say anything. I wonder how obvious our attraction is to everyone. If Annie noticed immediately, then there's no way Tyler wouldn't.

As Mimi sets our slices of pie in front of us, Everleigh places her hand on my thigh under the table. I gulp and wonder if she's purposely trying to test my limits in front of her family. Gemma comes around and scoops ice cream onto everyone's plate. If Tyler knew how close his sister's hand was to my dick right now, he'd lose his shit. I sit as still as I can, trying not to draw attention or let on how affected I am by her touch.

When Mimi returns from the kitchen, Everleigh's hand disappears. She's definitely trying to provoke me, and the fact that she's doing it with family around makes me think she likes having power over me.

After dessert, Mimi pulls out old photo albums of Tyler and Everleigh, mostly from when Everleigh was in high school, and tells me stories about each one.

"She's always skipped to her own beat," Gemma says as she watches next to me. "Look at this outfit! And here's Tyler before boot camp! Wasn't he a stud?" She giggles.

"Wow," I say, noticing the jeans he was wearing. "You look like you should be in a boy band."

"Thank God I grew out of that stage," he says with a humorless laugh.

"That's the boy I fell in love with all those years ago," Gemma gushes.

We look at more pictures until Scarlett starts to get fussy, and I know our night's coming to an end.

Everleigh starts yawning, and as predicted, we're soon at the front door, saying our goodbyes.

"Come see us anytime, Archer. Our home is your home," Mimi says, and Everleigh gives me a knowing *I told you so* look.

I've never felt so accepted, like I'm a part of a real family. I know Tyler and Everleigh didn't have the best childhood either, but their grandparents' love for them is evident.

She sends us home with a week's worth of leftovers, and I can't stop smiling at how welcoming and generous they were.

Once we're in the car, Everleigh faces me. "Did you have a good time?"

"Actually, I did. Thank you."

"For what?" she asks, confused.

"For inviting me and not treating me like an outsider."

"I'd never, Archer. You're one of us now—basically a Blackwood."

I'm sure she doesn't realize it, but her words are music to my ears.

However, it's just another reminder that Tyler sees me like a brother, and breaking that bond would ruin us both.

CHAPTER TWELVE

EVERLEIGH

ONLY TWO MORE DAYS UNTIL this year is over. I tend to get wild without apology every New Year's Eve. But right now, all I can think about is spending that night with Archer. I don't know if he'd agree to hang out with me. I might need a little liquid courage to work up the nerve to ask.

He knows that I can be a bit much at times, and considering we've almost crossed the line on several occasions, he might say no.

I've been slowly putting away Christmas decorations all week, so it won't be as taxing after the first. I went overboard, but I have no regrets. Every customer who walked through the door looked around and smiled.

It felt like I worked in a cute little shop inside of a Hallmark movie. I even ran into the handsome stranger who moved to my small town to save the day. Archer would roll his eyes if I told him that. And our happily ever after better not just end with a kiss. No, I want to lick that man from top to bottom.

Just as I'm helping Dana carry more shirts from the back, my phone dings with a text.

Gemma: Don't forget. Lunch at 11 on the dot!

Katie: I'll be there. My mom is watching the babies for me!

Everleigh: Yay! I set an alarm on my phone to alert me when I need to stop working and leave. Won't be late. Promise.

I laugh because they know me so well. On more than one occasion, I've nearly missed our lunch dates because I've gotten so caught up at work. But today, that ain't happening!

After I've boxed up one of the trees along with the ornaments, I make several trips to the storage area in the back. Before I can get too caught up in anything else, my lunch reminder alarm goes off.

I pass Lexie, who's carrying garland, while Dana handles the register.

"Oh hey, I'm heading out for lunch. I'll be back in an hour. If it gets really busy, can one of you text me, and I'll come back and help?"

Lexie laughs and waves me off. "We'll be fine! It's just one hour. Go have fun."

"Okay, okay," I say, grabbing my crossbody and make my way to the front of the store.

"Tell Archer I said hi!" she yells across the room. Heads turn and look at me with envy.

"I'm not meeting him." I shake my head and continue forward, kinda wishing I were. No telling how fast it would spread around town that we were dating if we started going out in public together. It's already gotten out that he lives with me. Us hooking up would be a rumor I for once wished were true. Hell, I'd *gladly* claim that one.

As I walk outside, daydreaming about Archer, I notice a black Dodge Charger parked by my car. My face contorts as two men come into view. They're dressed in suits and ties and look completely out of place. Their presence puts me on high alert, and I wonder if I scream loud enough if my employees would hear.

"Can I help you?" I ask, grabbing their attention. It's better to act fearless than to show any signs of weakness.

"Everleigh Blackwood?" the tall one asks.

"Who wants to know?" I try to keep a smile, but I can already tell by their demeanor that they're hard-asses.

"I'm Detective Ballard, and this is Detective Haven. We have some questions about Eric Hudson." They show their credentials, and I'm not sure if it puts me at ease or stresses me out more.

I look around, making sure no one is witnessing this. The last thing I need is for this to spread around town.

My attention focuses back on them.

"Okay, what about him?" I'm growing more impatient with each passing second. I literally have a couple of minutes to make it to the deli if I'm going to be on time. Sure, it's right down the street, but I was trying to be punctual for once in my life. Guess that's not happening today.

"It's been brought to our attention that you had a personal relationship with him, so we need to know where you were on the night of October twenty-second." Detective Haven's light blue eyes stare through me.

I'm so shocked by the question that I laugh. "You can't be serious."

Their reactions say otherwise.

Rolling my eyes, I huff and open the calendar app on my phone. The next day was Katie's baby shower. "I went home after working an eight-hour shift. I had an event the next morning for one of my best friends, so I stayed in."

Ballard flips open a small pocket notebook. "Can anyone confirm you went home?"

My patience is waning. "You could ask my dog. Considering I live alone, she's about the only one who knows I was there. I ate dinner, watched a little TV, then went to bed. Had to be at the venue at eight to start decorating."

"So, you don't have an alibi before eight o'clock the next day?"

I don't want to hear anymore because I know exactly what he's insinuating, and they're reaching at this point if I'm their best suspect. "Excuse me, what do you think I did? That I flew to Vegas to kill him, then made it home just in time to host a party the following day? That'd give me barely enough time."

He looks down at my left finger and sees it's bare. "*Ms. Blackwood, you're a person of interest for the murder of Eric Hudson. He was staying with you for a little while, wasn't he? You two had an affair?*"

"This is ridiculous. Maybe you should ask his wife to explain everything, considering she embarrassed me the next day in front of the entire town. If anyone would have a motive, it'd be *her*."

They exchange a look, then focus back on me.

Haven clears his throat. "His wife was here in Lawton Ridge?"

"Yes. Afternoon of the twenty-third. She decided to slap me

across the face for sleeping with her husband. Trust me, I had no idea he was married before then."

Probably came here to make a scene and an alibi for herself. If she didn't have anything to do with his murder, I'd be willing to bet she has an idea of who did.

"And what about—?"

"Sorry, but I have somewhere I need to be, and you've already slowed me down enough. I'm not answering any more questions without a lawyer present. I'm aware of my rights, and unless you're detaining me…" I look back and forth between them, and neither says anything. "Then have a good day, detectives."

Knowing they can't arrest me without the proper evidence, I hurry down the sidewalk enraged.

I check my phone and am already ten minutes late. Five minutes later, I make my way inside the deli and see my best friends seated by the window. They wave, and I'm trying really hard not to let those men ruin my day.

There's already a big glass of sweet tea waiting for me. I sit down in the booth next to Katie with a sigh.

"I win. You're buying my lunch," Gemma tells her.

"You two placed bets on if I would be on time, didn't you?" I glance at them.

"Well. We actually placed bets on how late you'd be." Gemma grins.

"I said five to ten minutes," Katie admits, and I stare at Gemma.

"I guessed fifteen to twenty." Gemma shrugs. "I know you too well."

Belinda greets me with a menu, but I don't take it. "Grilled cheese and tomato soup, please."

"Good choice." She nods with a grin, then walks away. The place is packed with the lunch rush.

"Someone piss on your avocado toast this morning?" Gemma finally asks because I'm being quieter than usual. Typically, I have a million things to discuss, but right now, my mind is racing.

Lowering my voice, I huff and tell them exactly what just happened outside of my shop. I repeat every word of the conversation, and I'm still as shocked as they look.

"I never thought I'd be a person of interest in a murder case," I finish with a sigh.

"What the hell?" Katie hisses, and concern is written on Gemma's face.

"Just because I had sex with the man doesn't mean I wanted him dead. He was actually a great lover, and I woulda hit it again." I wink. "I mean, well, if he were alive. May he rest in peace."

Katie chuckles. "I could just tell. It's always the quiet types, you know?"

Immediately, I think of Archer and how well he balances my personality. He's not my usual type, but he's quickly becoming the only man I want. Eric was nice and a great booty call, but there weren't sparks. He didn't take my breath away. There's no comparison between the two other than them both being my brother's friend.

"Tyler's going to flip his shit," Gemma says. "But maybe he can get Serena to help you? She's amazing."

"I know. And please don't tell my brother just yet. I'd love to be able to process it all before he starts playing bodyguard." I suck in a deep breath; my anxiety is starting to get the best of me.

"Everything's gonna be okay," Katie ensures. "The whole

town can vouch for seeing Eric's wife slap the blush right off your cheeks."

I roll my eyes. "Now is not the time for jokes."

"Oh, I wasn't joking." She laughs and bumps me with her elbow, trying to cheer me up.

"Bottom line is I need to figure out what I'm going to do. This is the last thing I want to be dealing with. I have big plans for the boutique this year, and I don't want that getting around and ruining my reputation."

"I don't blame you, and you know we wouldn't let that happen," Katie states.

"I wonder what really happened to Eric, though," Gemma mumbles.

"I've been thinking about this in true crime style and have tried to put the pieces together," I say.

Gemma lifts a brow.

"I think his wife suspected he was cheating, so she hired a private investigator. Otherwise, I don't know how else she would've found out. None of you knew until she blurted it out to the entire town. Anyway, when she got confirmation, she planned her ultimate revenge and waited for him to come home. It's a classic lover's scorned tale. Thousands of books and movies are out there with the same premise. Typically, the simplest answer is the right one. At least that's what all the crime documentaries I've watched taught me."

"You and your Crime TV." Gemma chuckles.

"But Eric went home in May, and he wasn't murdered until October," Katie points out.

"Right." I nod.

"Why would she wait so long to kill him?" Gemma asks.

"Hmm, okay. Maybe she confronted him, he apologized and promised to never do it again, then eventually he does.

That's her last straw, and she takes him out," I explain. "Though I really didn't see Eric as a cheater. Maybe it was a loveless marriage?"

"Tyler was shocked to hear he'd been married after his girlfriend passed last year, so maybe it was arranged?" Gemma suggests.

"Yes...like mafia-style," I add.

"And if that was the case, why would the wife kill him if they weren't in love?" Katie asks.

"And why would she come all the way here to confront you?" Gemma asks.

"Right, I'm not sure." I shrug, scratching my head. "I just know that I didn't do shit to him. Except give him multiple orgasms."

Gemma snickers. "I need to be there when you tell the detectives that one."

Scowling, I roll my eyes. "What would even be *my* motive?"

"Crazy jealous mistress is sick of waiting around for her man to leave his wife, so she takes things into her own hands and kills him. Now neither of them can have him," Gemma concludes all dramatically. "You flew there Friday evening, murdered him in the heat of passion, then flew home on the red-eye so you could make it back in time for the party and have an alibi. The perfect crime." Gemma smiles proudly at her theory.

"Probably what the detectives have already concluded." Katie bursts out laughing as I glare at her, unamused.

"I think *you're* the ones who've been watching too much Crime TV," I tell them.

"His wife is probably a person of interest too, because how else would they know about your affair? She's probably trying to put the heat on you and off her," Katie says just as Belinda walks up with our food on a tray. She sets it down and passes out our dishes. Our detective talk is quickly dropped.

"Oh my goodness, Belinda! I forgot to say how excited I am for you and Jerry!" I mention, remembering Gemma told me the good news on Christmas Eve.

Belinda blushes. "Thank you. I'm such a lucky lady."

Gemma smiles from ear to ear, and I know she's just as excited. After her mom passed away, she was convinced her dad would never marry again. Over two decades later, he met Belinda, and that all changed. They've been dating for a few years, and they're the cutest couple.

"I just hope I find love like that one day." I look around the table. "Well, like all of you lovebirds." I playfully pout and pick up my spoon.

"Honey, you will. You might already have," she says, giving me a knowing look, and for a brief second, I wonder if she can read my mind. "Y'all need anything else over here?"

"No, ma'am," Katie tells her, and Belinda leaves.

I look at what they got and chuckle. "Tomato soup and grilled cheese for everyone, huh?"

Katie snorts. "It took everything inside me not to burst out laughing when you ordered the same as us."

"I love you two. I seriously dunno what I'd do without you," I admit because they're more like my sisters than friends.

"We love you too," Katie says.

"Wouldn't want to live this crazy life without you two by my side," Gemma adds.

We eat in silence for a minute.

"Other than the detectives, have you noticed anything else weird going on?" Gemma asks.

I swallow hard, feeling the lump form in my throat as I think about the past few weeks. Deciding to tell them, I exhale. "Well, I have seen this all-black Escalade around town. I've felt like someone's following me, but I don't know if I'm just being paranoid after what happened to Tyler and Noah. It could've been those detectives, but I have no idea. It's just been odd."

Katie drops her fork. "I've seen that vehicle around too."

"The first time, I saw it parked on the street outside of my house. Then the second time was in front of my shop after our photo shoot."

"That wasn't that long ago." Gemma's brows furrow.

"I know. I wonder if the psycho wife is having me followed. Would make sense as to why those detectives showed up today. Either she killed him and she wants to kill me next or she's trying to find a way to plant evidence to get me in trouble."

"It could be nothing," Gemma encourages, but I notice the worry in her eyes.

When we're halfway through our soups and sandwiches, Katie softly clears her throat. "So, you gonna tell us what's really going on with you and Archer?"

I shrug, but my adrenaline rushes. "Oh, not much."

Gemma narrows her eyes. "Lies from the pits of hell."

Katie laughs, and I join her.

"He's hot," I admit, but God knows it's much deeper than that.

When I think about Archer, my whole body heats, just like it is right now. The way he looks at me is hypnotizing. Not to mention how good it feels sleeping next to him every night, but that's another thing I'll keep buried deep inside.

"You know I'm not the type of girl who kisses and tells," I state matter-of-factly.

"Bullshit," Katie hisses.

At the same time, Gemma asks, "Wait, so you've kissed?"

"Yes…or no." I make a zipper motion over my mouth and throw away the key.

"Oh, come on," Gemma nearly begs, but I keep my lips sealed tight.

While we haven't kissed, there have been many *almost* kisses.

Right now, I'd love to tell my two best friends every little detail, but I can't risk Tyler finding out that I've caught feelings.

My heart knows who it wants in ways I've never felt before, regardless of how wrong it is.

CHAPTER THIRTEEN

ARCHER

"Avocado toast?" Everleigh asks when I come into view. She's trying to tease the hell out of me in that white shirt that's as thin as paper, and fuck, it's working.

"No thanks," I say, grabbing a protein shake from the fridge. "I have a client at seven and can't be late," I admit, checking the time on my phone.

"Do you want me to drive you?" Everleigh asks.

"Nah. I'm gonna walk and drink this at the same time," I say. "Kill two birds or whatever."

"I insist," she tells me. "I haven't started breakfast and could go for a donut before I need to get dressed for work. I can drop you off on the way."

I smile, knowing she's not going to give me a choice. "Okay, but only because you *insisted*."

Everleigh grabs her keys and slides on her slippers. After she remote starts her car, she grabs a jacket and gives me the perfect view of her hard nipples.

As she's driving out of her neighborhood, she turns to me. "Before you crack open that nasty shake, can I tempt you with a glazed donut? There's nothing like having sugar for breakfast."

I snort. "Well, when you put it like that..."

She grins wide and parks in front of the bakery. We walk in, and the woman at the cash register smiles when she sees Everleigh. "Oh my God, do you just wake up looking cute?"

Yep, I want to say but keep it to myself.

"Thanks, Lori, you're too sweet." Everleigh dips down and looks at all the pastries in the case. "I'll have a chocolate-covered donut and a chocolate-filled one. He'll have..." She looks at me, tapping her finger across her plump, kissable lips. "A blueberry cake and a raspberry-filled one. I know how he likes to taste sweet things."

The girl looks at me for confirmation, and I nod. "Fine with me. Apparently, we have a donut aficionado here."

"Damn right." Everleigh leans into me.

"Do you want them in the same bag?" Lori asks.

"Separate, please," Everleigh confirms.

I hear the clearing of a throat behind me and turn to see Tyler.

"Mornin'." He looks back and forth between us, noticing how close we're standing.

Everleigh immediately creates space, and I straighten my stance. I have no idea how long he's been there or if he witnessed the blatant flirting. Though I've done nothing wrong, it's obvious Everleigh was skirting the line.

"Guess we had the same thought," Tyler speaks up.

"I'm surprised you want sweets for breakfast," Everleigh says.

"Actually, Gemma asked me to pick up some for her," he admits. "Happy wife, happy life."

Everleigh snorts. "That's right. You better take care of my bestie. Also, she likes Bavarian cream. Surprise her with it."

Everleigh pays, and we're handed our bags.

"Really? How did I not know that?" Tyler chuckles as other people enter. "See ya at work," he tells me, then not so casually pats my shoulder as we pass him.

"Headed there now." I nod and exit, hoping like hell he's not going to kick my ass for whatever he thinks is happening between Everleigh and me.

Once we're in the car, it's quiet, and I wonder what Everleigh's thinking.

"Thanks for the donuts," I tell her when she stops in front of the gym. "You actually did choose one of my favorites."

"Yeah?" Her voice raises an octave. "Don't tell me…it was the raspberry-filled one, right?"

I shake my head and smirk. "Blueberry cake."

"Damn. Almost!"

"So close," I say, winking.

"Story of my life. Anyway, have a great day, Archer. Enjoy your sugar crash this afternoon." I feel like she wants to say something more but doesn't.

I shake my head and chuckle. "Thanks, you too." I get out of the car and take a big bite of one as I head inside.

Ten minutes later, Trevor arrives, and we get started. After our warm-up, we box a round.

"Throw all your weight into it," I direct, showing Trevor exactly how to do a side hook. He bounces around, putting the training he's done the past month to the test.

I quickly move from side to side, extending a punch and then another. Trevor ducks, and his gloved fist connects with my cheek. The bell rings, and we climb over the rope. He's smiling wide and stands proudly.

"Good job, man." We take off our gloves, and I give him a high five.

"You think so?"

"Yeah, keep at it, and you'll be able to enter competitions by the summer if that's still your goal."

His expression is serious. "It's all I've ever wanted, and I'm determined to make it happen. Especially with you as my coach."

"Would love to see it."

"Same time tomorrow?" Trevor asks, wiping the sweat from his brow.

"Yeah." I nod. "I got you down for the month."

"Awesome, thanks!" He grabs his gear bag and leaves.

Tyler enters, smiling. "He's doin' great already. But how are you doin'?"

A big cheesy grin meets my lips. "This is the best job I've ever had."

"Love to hear it. Just wanted to make sure. I mean, if you were having second thoughts, I'd respect that too."

"Hell no. I genuinely like it here. The town, the gym, the people. It's everything I never knew I needed in life but did. Funny because if you would've asked me to move somewhere like this years ago, I would've not only said no but fuck no. Weirdly enough, it already feels like home."

"Good to hear, man. I know how important it is to have the proper time to focus on yourself without any outside distractions. For me, the gym opening was all I focused my energy on. Noah helped me remodel the place. But after a while, he realized that he enjoyed working with his hands and building things. I guess what I'm saying is if you find something else you want to do in life that you're more passionate about, I support it."

"Thanks, Tyler. That means a lot."

He clears his throat. "So how's living with Everleigh?"

I knew this conversation was coming.

"It's fine," I say.

"You two seemed close this morning." His intense gaze pins me in place.

My heart races, but I try to keep my breathing steady. Any time I think about her, the thoughts consume me. My silence draws on, not sure what the correct answer is, and he eventually speaks up.

"While I don't want to sound like a dick, I still have to protect my sister. No matter how old we get, I'll never stop being her big brother. Rushing into any relationship, but especially with her, is a bad idea. She isn't quite ready for the whole marriage and babies lifestyle, if ya know what I mean."

"Oh, I've noticed." It's no wonder she's the last of her friends to do either.

He continues, "I'd hate to see one of my close friends get hurt, and I don't want to see my little sister heartbroken."

"I know." I meet his eyes.

Though he laughs, he adds, "And I don't want to have to punch your face in if you were the cause of it."

I roll my eyes but agree with the sentiment.

"I wouldn't do anything to make you that pissed," I confirm with Everleigh front and center in my mind. We've grown close, and I can't deny that. She makes me laugh and doesn't let me stay inside my shell for too long without calling me out. I wish I could make her happy, but I've never had a serious relationship. And while she makes me want the idea of *more*, I'd probably mess it up.

Tyler interrupts my thoughts. "Anyway, I'm glad you're happy here and liking it so far."

"Yeah. It's not half as bad as I was anticipating," I reaffirm with a grin.

Smith waves at Tyler, and he excuses himself.

The air in the room feels thick as I think about everything. Right now, as hard as it is, I know I need to force her away. Everleigh has admitted she has issues when it comes to dating as well.

Hurting her would be one of the biggest regrets of my life right next to betraying my best friend. The thought makes me feel guilty. Everleigh has burrowed herself under my skin, and I don't know how I'm going to wash the thoughts of her away. But damn, I'm going to have to try.

Needing to get out of here, I leave the gym before my next client arrives.

The temperature has dropped to the fifties. The sweat on my back feels cold in the weather, but I keep walking.

Eventually, I pass the boutique and know Everleigh's inside working. I'd love to go in and say hello, but I don't want to give her the wrong impression, not while I'm already questioning everything. Pulling my eyes away, I keep moving forward until I'm standing outside the coffee shop downtown.

Smells of peppermint and chocolate waft through the air when I walk in and scan the menu.

A redheaded woman greets me with a smile.

"Whatcha havin', sugar?"

"Just a regular coffee."

She playfully rolls her eyes as if she's offended. "Out of all these magical drink choices I have, you order that."

I can tell she's joking by her tone.

Seconds later, she pours it in a to-go cup, then hands it over.

"Thank you. How much do I owe you?"

"It's on the house." She flashes a wink.

I thank her again, then tuck a five-dollar bill in her tip jar.

On the way back to the gym, I take a sip, but it's too hot to keep drinking.

When I look up, I see the same black Escalade parked on the side of the road. My heart races, and I pick up my pace. If Krystal is behind this, I'm determined to find out. I tightly grip my cup and break into a jog. Twenty feet from it, the engine starts and zooms off.

"What the fuck?" I hiss, convinced I'm being followed.

When I walk inside the gym, my adrenaline courses through my veins as I try to put the pieces together. But I force myself to shake it off before my next client arrives. The lesson goes by quickly, and so do my other sessions. For the rest of the day, I'm unsettled.

The mood sits heavily on my shoulders as I walk home with my eyes wide open. I'm determined to find out who the hell is following me and why.

When I walk in, Sassy immediately greets me with a bark. I let her out, and she runs around until she grows bored.

I take a shower, wanting to clear my mind. When I get out, I check to see if Everleigh is home yet and then see a text from her.

Everleigh: Staying late to put up a new shipment of inventory. Feel free to eat leftovers or make whatever you want!

It's not out of the ordinary for her to stay a few hours after close. I contemplate waiting for her, but when my stomach growls, I decide to heat some food. As I eat, my mind races with Tyler's words. The truth of it pierces through me like a knife, and what I know I have to do nearly guts me.

Once I start yawning, I decide to go to bed. After I walk into my room, there's a bit of hesitation, but I force myself to lock the door.

Tyler's right.

He knows us both better than we know each other.

I lie in bed and stare at the ceiling. The last thing I want to do is hurt her feelings, but it's inevitably going to happen. I try to push the thoughts away and tell myself it's what I have to do before I hurt her worse.

Creating healthy boundaries and locking her out of my room and heart is the best thing for us both.

Isn't it?

CHAPTER FOURTEEN

EVERLEIGH

COUNTING inventory and putting up new items typically takes me hours. It consists of unboxing clothes, checking every single item, then steaming out wrinkles before hanging them up. Quality control is important to me, so I personally put my eyes and hands on every single hem.

Lexie volunteered to help, which is why I won't be stuck here till midnight. She enjoys opening the boxes just as much as I do, especially since they have no idea what I've ordered until it arrives.

This shipment is more winter clothes with sweaters of different thicknesses and winter leggings even though Alabama doesn't get that cold.

"I love these so much," Lexie says, holding up a pair of wool-lined leggings.

"Take those home with you."

"You're sure?" She gives me a wide-eyed expression.

"Absolutely. That way, when you're asked about them, you can give your opinion." I wink.

"Oh my goodness, thank you. You're seriously the best boss I've ever had!"

I laugh. "I've got to award my manager somehow."

"That's for damn sure," she tells me with a laugh as we continue unpackaging shirts.

By the time everything's in place, I look up at the clock and see it's just past eight thirty. My stomach is growling nonstop. I hurry and sweep the floor, then throw all the plastic wrappers in the trash. Lexie and I lock up and walk out together.

"Thanks again for your help," I say again, waving goodbye.

"Any time." She grins. "Appreciate the leggings. I'm wearing them tomorrow during my shift."

"Do it!" I chuckle, then get in my car.

As I drive home, all I can think about is snuggling into Archer's body and him holding me close. It's a dangerous game we're playing. I should stop it before it ends badly, but I don't have the strength to. I'm not the best at relationships, but I'd try for Archer—if he'd give us a chance.

He makes me want more than just a hookup, someone to settle down with and build a life—something that's never crossed my mind before.

I park in my driveway, then look in the rearview mirror to make sure the street is clear of suspicious vehicles before getting out.

Ever since the detectives came and talked to me, I've been jumpy and am convinced someone's tailing me. I force the thoughts away and go inside the house. All the lights are turned off except for the Christmas tree. It casts a warm glow against the walls and creates a homey atmosphere that I love so much. It always makes me a little sad to take it down.

Knowing Archer's already asleep, I make a sandwich, then

quickly shower. Once I'm ready for bed, I go to Archer's room like usual. When I turn the knob, it doesn't open. I slowly twist it again and confirm that he's really locked me out.

My smile fades, and it feels like a punch to the gut when I think I hear a woman's voice on the other side.

"Wow. Okay, then," I mumble to myself, then decide I need a glass of wine. I pull the merlot from the cabinet, and when I turn, Sassy's at my feet. Needing some fresh air, I leave everything on the counter and lead her out.

She bolts forward, immediately barking and growling. Squinting, I notice a tall, dark silhouette and scream. Before I can see their face, they take off running, disappearing into the shadows. Sassy continues barking as I try to catch my breath and calm my racing heart.

Moments later, the back porch light flicks on, and Archer walks out. "What happened?"

"There was someone out here. I think it was a man by the height and built, but I'm not sure." I blow out a slow breath as he comes closer. "They bolted that way," I explain, pointing in the direction.

"I'll be right back," Archer says, then crosses the yard to walk around the house to the front.

Sassy finally finds a spot to pee, then we go back into the house and wait for Archer.

"Whoever it was is long gone," he returns, shaking his head. "I think I heard a car speed off."

I immediately think of the black SUV.

Archer gently grabs my elbow and pulls me in. "You're shaking."

"It looked like he was near my bedroom window," I say.

Leading me to sit down at the breakfast bar, he puts some water in a kettle. "Tea?"

"Archer, you don't have to do this. You can go back to your guest." I stand to take over, but he gives me a puzzled look.

"You think I have someone in my room?"

I freeze, embarrassed by my assumption. "I thought I heard a woman's voice. Isn't that why you locked the door?"

Archer crosses his arms over his broad chest and sighs. "I was talking to my sister. And that's not why I locked the door."

I narrow my eyes as the elephant in the room appears. Instead of blowing it off or making a joke at my own expense, like I usually would, I say something. I need to *hear* him say what I already know. "Then why?"

"Everleigh." His voice drops, and I hate how my body reacts to him. "I just don't think it's a good idea that we sleep in the same bed anymore."

"Oh. Alright." I nod as my heart thumps erratically. I'm feeling more deflated as reality sets in, and I wish I had that bottle of wine instead of the tea he offered. I won't pursue someone who doesn't want me back, but I can at least drink away my sorrows.

As if he can read my mind, he continues, "It's not like that. It's just Tyler said some things today that make sense regarding you and me." He meets my eyes, and I know exactly what he's referring to—us being together.

A furious laugh escapes me. "Oh really? Like Tyler is the relationship expert here. Gimme a break. I hate to break it to you, but he's not, regardless of how much he thinks us being involved is a bad idea."

"He just wants the best for us both. I genuinely believe that," he admits, and I sigh harshly.

"I'm an adult who can make her own decisions. I'm sick of him interfering with my life. If it were up to Tyler, I'd never date anyone and would die a virgin. It's exhausting to constantly remind him I'm *not* a child."

"What if we *are* a mistake for each other?" he asks.

"Then it'd be a mistake I'd love to make. What's that saying about loving and losing, then not experiencing it at all? Well, that," I say, confidently, then hear a car door outside and jump. Then the tea kettle howls, and I nearly scream. I'm still shaken up from what happened, and now I have to deal with his rejection.

Archer looks over at me, then pours some hot water in a mug with some Earl Grey. He even puts a spoonful of honey in it too, just the way I like it.

Carefully, he places it in front of me, then sits down. "What's going on with you? You seem really jumpy and paranoid."

I don't know how to bring it up, but I find my courage and let it all out. "I'm worried about the black SUV I keep seeing around town. I have a feeling whoever was in my backyard had something to do with the Escalade. On top of that, two detectives stopped me yesterday to ask me questions about—"

"*Detectives?*" He raises a brow. "You didn't tell me that."

I steep my drink. "Yes. Apparently, I'm a person of interest in Eric's murder. They wanted to know where I was the night he was killed."

He places his hand on mine for a moment before pulling away. "That's crazy. You're innocent, so you have nothing to worry about. They're just doing their job and following all possible leads. Also, I truly believe that Escalade is actually following me."

My eyes go wide. "What? Why?"

He releases a breath, then closes his eyes tight before opening them. "I think it's Chad's family. They weren't happy

I was being released. Well, more specifically, his sister. There was a whole social media tirade. Anyway, I think she hired someone, or she herself is following me," he admits.

"For what?"

He shrugs, just as frustrated as I am with this. "Not sure. To scare me, to hurt me, to fuck with me. Who knows."

Silence passes, but I'm not convinced he's the one being followed after those detectives approached me.

"I don't want to put you in any kind of danger, Everleigh. It's why I locked my door. That's why I don't know if I should stay in Lawton Ridge."

My heart drops as a knot forms in my stomach. "That SUV could be following me. Neither of us knows for sure. At this point, I think it's safer to stay close, at least until we figure out who's the target."

Archer meets my eyes with a slight nod. "You're right. I don't want to leave if you're being followed. I'm torn because I refuse to put you in harm's way. I couldn't live with myself if something happened to you because of me, Everleigh."

"I feel the same. That's why we need each other."

He flashes a small smile, and I yawn. As soon as I finish my tea, Archer rinses my mug. He meets my eyes, then holds out his hand.

Without hesitation, I take it as he leads me to his room. I stop before entering.

Archer turns and looks at me, the corner of his lips tilting up in a cocky grin. "Will you sleep with me tonight?"

I'm still so shaken up that I know I'd feel safer being next to him, even if we're fighting an internal battle of how close we should be.

But selfishly, I agree.

"Remember, this was *your* idea," I tell him as we walk in.

With a smirk, Archer strips down to his boxers and gets under the covers. Then he pats the bed and waits for me to join him. Rolling onto my side, I let out a breath, then close my eyes. Our backs are facing, but within seconds, he turns and blankets me in his warmth.

I softly breathe out, imagining he's mine, and almost instantly fall asleep.

CHAPTER FIFTEEN

ARCHER

I CAN'T BELIEVE it's already New Year's Eve. The first one I'll celebrate in five years.

The gym's insanely busy this morning as people start their routine a day early. Since Christmas, people have joined the gym by the handfuls. Tyler has coined it as the *Resolution Rush*.

After my last client of the day, I go up front and order a smoothie.

Tyler walks up, looking exhausted.

"You okay?" I ask.

"It's barely three, and I'm ready for bed. I dunno if I'll make it to midnight this year."

I chuckle with a shrug. "Dad life."

"Exactly. Any big plans tonight?"

I shake my head, grabbing my drink off the counter. "Nope."

He gives me a weary look. "Everleigh usually *always* goes out."

"I'm not sure what she's doing. We haven't really talked about it," I say truthfully.

Things have been somewhat awkward since the night I locked her out of my room and told her my concerns about what Tyler said. Even though nothing has really changed in our sleeping arrangement, there's an invisible line we know we can't cross.

"Well, if you get bored, you can always come hang out with us. But be warned, we'll probably fall asleep on the couch once Scarlett is in bed. Way before the ball drops."

I chuckle. "Thanks for the offer. Not sure what I'll be in the mood for. I'm gonna go home and take a nap since it's still early, then decide."

"Sounds like a good idea. Go out and have some fun," he suggests. "Just responsible fun."

I laugh at his fatherly tone. "See ya later," I tell him, then grab my stuff.

After I tell everyone goodbye, I walk home. I'm saving up for a car, but it's not so bad walking since Everleigh lives less than a mile from the downtown district. Plus, it adds more activity points to my week for the Apple watch challenge we're doing, and I might actually win for once.

Once I walk in the door, I take Sassy out the back, then jump in the shower. My eyes are so heavy that when I lie down on the couch, I end up falling asleep.

It's not until a few hours later when Everleigh comes in that I wake up.

I hear a clicking noise and see Everleigh has her Polaroid camera in one hand and a photo in the other. I glance down and see Sassy snuggled in beside me. We're two peas in a pod.

"Sorry, couldn't help myself. That was a cute moment to capture."

I sit up, and Sassy repositions herself. We must've slept hard because I feel so disoriented.

"Did you just get home?"

"Yeah. We were busy as hell today."

"It's been crazy all week." I run my fingers through my hair, then stand and stretch before making some coffee.

Everleigh takes Sassy out and returns. She watches me and leans against the counter. "What're your plans tonight? Considering you're making coffee after six, I'd say you're stayin' up?"

Her gaze slides up my body and lingers on my abs before meeting my eyes. I give her a look, letting her know I just caught her eye-fucking me. She does it when she can, and I can't say I'm not guilty of the same thing.

It's hard to ignore when the attraction between us runs so damn deep.

"Come out with me tonight," she blurts out, just as I'm pouring my mug full.

"I don't think that's a good idea," I admit, even if it pains me to do so. The defeat I saw the other night when I locked her out isn't present. Everleigh shrugs like she's not bothered by my response.

"Okay, then. Suit yourself. But I was thinkin' that since all my other friends are home with their kiddos, you and I could go out of town. Maybe have a little fun at one of my favorite places, then crash at a hotel, but if you want to stay here and snuggle with Sassy all night, that's fine too. I'm sure I can find someone else to accompany me." Everleigh unlocks her phone that was sitting on the counter. The thought of her going anywhere with another man frustrates the fuck out of me, not including the jealousy that follows closely behind.

"I could text Brian. He's a baseball player. Or maybe Jesse. He's a drummer, really good with his sticks too. Oh, I bet Daryl and Zach would be game. They're twins, by the way, who are really into role-playing. Hmm...which one would show me the best time?" she contemplates, tapping her nails.

She's waiting for a reaction, but I wouldn't put it past her to really text someone. Any man would be an idiot to tell her no.

I shrug, then clear my throat to grab her attention. "Why not text them all? Have a big ole orgy?"

"Oh, come on, that should've worked!" Everleigh pushes out her bottom lip. "What if I promised to keep my hands above your waist at all times?"

A bark of laughter escapes me, but I can't deny her. Hell, I can't deny myself the chance to spend more time with her, especially away from Lawton Ridge.

"*Okay, okay.* I'll go with you."

She yelps and wraps her arms around my neck. "Yes! We're gonna have so much fun!"

"Why do I have a feeling I'll be eating my words later?"

"Ha-ha," she muses. "Give me an hour to get ready, please. Then we'll head out. Bring a change of clothes 'cause we're staying out all night."

"Sounds like a plan. I should probably change too."

"Nah. Go like that," she tells me, memorizing my abs before looking at the waistband of my joggers. "I'll be ready soon."

"Looking forward to it." I take a sip of my coffee when she goes into her room. After I've finished my coffee, I put on some of the clothes Everleigh gave me for Christmas.

When I return to the living room, she walks out and looks me up and down. "Nice choice. You've got style."

"You mean, a *stylist*."

"Same difference." Everleigh lets Sassy out one last time

before grabbing her purse that's just big enough to fit her phone, debit card, and ID. She's wearing tight dark jeans with little rips in the knees that hug her perfect ass. Her blouse shows off just enough cleavage to make you want more. Right now, in those high heels, she looks good enough to eat. And she knows it.

"You look beautiful," I say after she catches me gawking.

Her cheeks redden. "Thank you, glad you think so."

Once we're in the car and heading out of town, Everleigh glances over at me. "You're gonna love this place. It's only an hour away, and unlike anything you've ever experienced before. Oh, and I already booked us a hotel that's within walking distance too."

"You do this a lot?" I ask. Though I wonder what kind of wild things Everleigh's done in her past, I also don't want to hear about her being with other men. I'm shocked she was able to get a room at the last minute.

"I like to have a good time," she confirms. "Since most of my friends are responsible adults who are married with kids, I often go out alone. Meet up with people online."

"Online?" My brows shoot up to my hairline. "That sounds dangerous. You never know what kind of psycho you could meet."

She laughs. "Oh, I've already met a few. It's just really hard to find single people in Lawton Ridge. Plus, I don't want my personal business spreading around town, which is why I prefer to leave."

"It's kinda nice knowing everyone, though."

"Yeah, but it can be a nightmare too. When I'd get in trouble at school, my grandparents would know before the last bell rang. It's just hard to keep secrets around here."

I smirk, thinking about a young Everleigh causing all sorts

of havoc for her teachers. I can only imagine how much of a handful she was.

"Then there was this time when I needed a pregnancy test because I was late. Spoiler alert, it was stress-related. Anyway, I had to order it online because I knew if I dared to get it from the grocery store, the rumor mill would start before I even peed on the stick. So, there's also that. It seems charming, and most times, it is unless you want to keep things private. Then everyone's up in your beeswax."

"Yeah, I guess I never thought about those sorts of things. Thankfully, we don't have anything to hide," I tell her, the words lingering on my lips while I try to bury my feelings.

It doesn't take long before we arrive at the club. The parking lot is packed, so Everleigh and I check into the hotel first, then walk over. We wait in line outside, and the cool air swirls around us. As soon as Everleigh shivers, I wrap my arm around her, knowing she loves my body heat. She looks at me and flashes a smile, her ruby-red lips taunting me. Eventually, it's our turn to go in.

I'm not sure what I expected when I walked in, but it definitely wasn't a country bar. I've been to a lot of different places in Vegas, but this is on another level. A dance floor occupies the middle, and a bull-riding area is across the way. I can hear high heels and boots shuffling against the wooden floor as people line dance. In the back are pool tables and what looks like darts. It's incredible.

"You like it?" she asks enthusiastically, and I think I hear her Southern drawl thicken. It's sexy as fuck.

"Love it!" I shout over the music, placing my hand on the small of her back as we sit at the bar. I can't help but want to be close to her and let every man in here know she's with me. She's by far the sexiest woman in this saloon, and although we never established we were exclusively dancing with each other, I'm not sure I can watch someone else's hands grab her waist. I've never been much of the jealous type, but when it comes to Everleigh, I selfishly want her all to myself.

The bartender comes over and immediately starts flirting with her.

"What're ya havin', *beautiful*?" He cocks a brow after blatantly staring at her tits.

Everleigh leans in closer to him and smirks. "What *should* I be having?"

My heart rate increases as I sit quietly, trying to act unfazed. If she's trying to make me jealous, it's working.

"For you, sweetheart? A screamin' orgasm," he tries to mumble seductively in her ear, but I overhear him. Watching someone with no game is sad. I wonder how many times he's already used that cheap pick-up line tonight.

Everleigh laughs and politely plays into it. "In that case, I'll take two."

I can't help but think back to the night her bed broke, wishing I'd been the one inside her, hearing *her* screaming orgasm.

"What about you, buddy?" His demeanor changes when he realizes she's not alone.

"Oh, I'll take a blow job," I say, straight-faced. An unspoken conversation flows between us, and I think he realizes I'm not amused by his flirting with Everleigh. With a head nod, he turns on his heels and makes our drinks.

Everleigh snickers. "Why didn't you just say so? Could've helped you with that myself."

I stare at her, unamused by her giving this asshole her attention. Though I've learned quickly that Everleigh is a little flirt.

"Loosen up," she says, pinching my side and forcing me to squirm. "I want you to have fun with me."

"I always do," I admit.

A beautiful smile sweeps across her plump lips.

The bartender arrives with our drinks, and I pay.

Everleigh looks at the whipped cream on my shot. "I kinda want a blow job now too. That looks good."

"It's all yours," I offer, sliding it over. I only ordered it to make a fucking point. If she's off-limits to me, she's off-limits to *everyone* in here. Next, I order a whiskey straight-up from the other bartender.

"Let's make a toast," Everleigh insists, holding both of her shots up, and I lift mine. "To friends. To love. To screamin' orgasms and blow jobs."

"Abso-fucking-lutely." We click our glasses together and suck them down. Then she shoots down the other.

"Want another?" I ask.

"Nah, I want to dance."

I shake my head. "Uh, I don't dance."

"You do when you're with me." Everleigh grabs my hand and forces me to the center of the room, where the lights are lowered. She places it on her waist, then interlocks her fingers with my other hand. "Follow my lead."

I can't help but smile as we make our way around the room in flow with all the other couples.

"You lied! You can two-step just fine."

"I have a good teacher," I taunt.

"Yeah, right."

I take her hand, twirl her around, and watch her face light up.

"You're basically a pro!" she squeals.

Everleigh comes back and wraps her arms around my neck.

"My sister loved to dance," I finally admit. "And she forced me to practice with her."

"I knew it. Most guys who really can't end up crushing my feet and looking like a tumbling mess."

The song ends, and the next is a slow one. I pull Everleigh to my chest, and she looks up at me with fire in her eyes. We sway to the music without saying a word, and it's nice. My mind wanders, and I wonder if we could make a relationship work. Between the reasons it can't, I like to think there's at least one why it could. The mood turns somber and serious, and I suggest we play pool when another slow one starts.

"Yeah," she says, stopping the waitress on the way to order a double shot of tequila.

We head into the game room area and wait for a table. Somehow, Everleigh sweet-talks some guys into letting us play after their round is over. I'm not the only one under her magical spell tonight because she's the center of attention.

"Have you played a lot?" She grabs a cue stick and rubs chalk over the tip.

I shrug. "I've won a few games or so."

She tilts a brow at me. "Are you a pool shark or something?"

I laugh. "No. Are you?"

"We'll see." She waggles her brows. "You wanna break the balls?"

"Go ahead," I tell her, knowing she's been breaking mine all night long. Rather, for *weeks*.

"Fatal mistake." She leans over, giving me the perfect view down her shirt. I move behind her so the temptation is gone, but that's when she bends over and pushes her ass in the air.

The top of her red lace thong has me adjusting my dick. Maybe playing pool was a bad idea. Next time, we're playing Chutes and Ladders at home fully clothed. Turtlenecks for everyone.

"I'm solids," she announces, walking around the table like she owns it while I chalk my cue. "We calling pockets or no?"

"Nah." I shrug.

"Mistake number two," she says, sinking four of her balls in the pocket.

I pop my wrists and take my turn. One stripe falls in, then another, and another, until we're even.

She gasps. "Are you fuckin' kidding me?"

I shoot her a wink, and she narrows her eyes.

When I only have two balls left on the table, she comes and stands next to me. "Glad we didn't play strip pool."

"Mm, now that would've been interesting." I slide my eyes up and down her body, the alcohol giving me too much courage. Being like this with her is just too damn easy. And too damn tempting.

I pull the stick back, and the white ball strikes against the yellow solid. It doesn't go in like I'd hoped.

"Yes!" She unapologetically fist pumps.

"You really are competitive at everything, aren't you?" I ask as she moves around to face me from the other side.

"Absolutely, and trust me when I say…" She straightens up, slowly sliding her eyes up and down my body. "I *always* win and get exactly what I want."

"I don't even doubt that." I swallow hard, secretly hoping I'm on that list. From all the signals she's thrown, I certainly am. I'm not imagining what we have. It's real as fuck.

"Now, I'm not gonna go easy on you," she mocks.

I'm realizing quickly that spending time with her like this is dangerous because it makes me crave more of this.

Like she's a pro, she announces her pocket, and the eight ball drops right in.

"Now, who'd be naked if we were strippin'?"

I smirk. "Hopefully both of us."

"Oh, I like that idea." She pops a brow.

We play another round, and she destroys me again.

The party favors are passed out ten minutes before midnight, and we watch the giant digital clock hanging above the bar.

Everleigh moves beside me, grabbing my hand as we countdown with the crowd. As soon as the clock strikes midnight, the band begins to play "Auld Lang Syne." Sounds of noisemakers fill the room as I pull Everleigh against me.

"Happy New Year, Everleigh," I whisper as her lips slightly part.

"Happy New Year," she says, studying my mouth intently.

I know damn well what's about to happen. The air in the room grows heavy as I slowly brush my thumb across her cheek. She shudders as I carefully tip up her chin and stare into her gorgeous blue eyes. Slowly, they flutter closed.

"Don't move," I whisper, doing what I've been dreaming about for weeks. Gently, I slide my lips across hers, taking my time to taste her. The kiss deepens, her tongue wrangles with mine, and I lose myself in her. My fingers thread through her hair, and she moans against me as she clings to my waist. I wish this moment could last forever. It takes everything I have to pull away.

"I'm really regretting my promise about keeping my hands off you," she admits with beautifully swollen lips.

"I'm regretting *a lot* of things," I say hoarsely, wanting and *needing* more of her. Everleigh's a rip current, pulling me away from the shore, but all I can do is tread water. If I'm not careful, she'll take me completely under.

"So, why'd you kiss me?" she asks softly.

I brush a piece of hair behind her ear and gaze into her eyes. "The first person you encounter in a new year sets the tone for the rest of the year. I wanted to make sure ours was set." Then I add, "Turns out I might've set us up for blue balls."

"You mean blue *bean*."

"Oh man, I've never heard that one before. Sounds painful."

She lets out an infectious laugh, then leads me back to the dance floor. I have a feeling that neither of us is thinking about anything other than that kiss. An experience I'd like to have again.

An hour passes, and I know if we don't get out of here, we might not be able to walk back to the hotel. Plus, Everleigh's yawning from working all day.

"Ready?" I finally ask.

"Yeah," she tells me with fire in her eyes.

I lead her through the crowd, and she nearly trips in the parking lot. I catch her, though she's in a fit of laughter.

"The more I drink, the clumsier I get. The heels ain't helpin' either."

"Well, if I need to carry you, just let me know."

She squeezes my bicep and waggles her brows. "Noted. Also, I wonder how many women wish you'd say that to them."

The alcohol has made her lips a lot looser, which isn't saying much, considering she's so outspoken. "Not many," I tell her.

"You have no idea how wrong you are."

I scoff.

"Every damn day, I get questions about your relationship status because of those pictures I posted. You have no idea what it does to me when they drool all over you."

"Probably the same way I felt having that bartender hit on you. Too many guys look at you like they're hungry vultures and you're their prey."

She snorts. "And now you've officially started to sound like my brother."

I shake it off and force a smile although it wasn't meant that way. Right now is not the time to spill what my heart is feeling. When we're finally up in the room, we change our clothes. Though the room has two beds, she crawls into mine just like at home.

"Thanks, Archer," she whispers as I turn off the side lamp.

"For what?"

"For coming with me and not being a complete and utter creep. Most guys would've tried to bring me back to their room to do nothing more than have sex. With you…it's different."

I stare into her eyes, and my face softens.

As hard as it is to admit, I say, "We can't cross that line."

She closes her eyes, and a small smile plays on her lips. "Yeah, but it sure is fun to fantasize about."

If my heart was available, Everleigh would have it. But right now, Tyler's words continue to play on repeat in my mind.

Tonight, I shouldn't have kissed her, but the only regret I have is not doing it again. Boundaries—I need to find them again before I end up breaking her heart and disappointing one of my best friends.

CHAPTER SIXTEEN

EVERLEIGH

MONDAY MORNING COMES EARLY, but I was ready for it after a day of recuperating from New Year's Eve. At the beginning of each year, I try to wake up earlier, eat healthier, and focus on self-care. It lasts about a month, but I always give it a good hurrah even though I consistently fail.

When I get up to grind some beans, Archer's in the kitchen scrambling eggs and making toast. He even cut fruit and put them in little side bowls. Bonus, he already started the coffee.

"You made me breakfast too?" My smile widens.

He nods proudly. "Of course."

"What's the occasion?" I ask as he hands me a mug of coffee just the way I like it.

"Breakfast is the most important meal of the day." He smirks, and I can't help but focus on his lips. Ever since our New Year's kiss, I haven't been able to think about anything else. When he holds me at night, I contemplate making a move, but I'd rather not know how it feels to be rejected by him.

"New year, new you, right?" He winks.

I wish he'd roughly rake his hands through my hair and devour my mouth. Instead, he hands me a plate with a fork.

"Maybe it's more like, new year, new *you*?" I challenge.

He sits in front of me, and sometimes, his gaze is so intense, my body just can't handle it.

"I guess it could be my year," he says. "It's gotta be better than the past five."

I smile. "I'm sure it will be. You've got a good job, a nice place to live, and a hot as fuck roommate. You're basically winning at life."

"All very, *very* true." There's a rasp in his voice, and his eyes darken with desire. I nearly choke on a grape, and Archer stands. "Are you okay?"

Coughing, I say, "I will be if you give me mouth-to-mouth."

A roar of laughter escapes him. "You'd need the Heimlich if you were choking."

I clear my throat and chuckle. "Can't blame a girl for tryin'."

He sits, and we finish eating, making small talk about our upcoming day.

"I have a bunch of one-hour sessions and some thirty-minute ones too. I'm gonna be exhausted tonight."

"Use my tub," I offer. "Let your muscles soak."

His brow lifts as if he forgot I had one. "I might take you up on that."

"You know, it's big enough for two," I taunt.

"Hmm. Might take you up on that too."

I nearly stop breathing and narrow my eyes at his teasing grin. "Don't mess with me."

"Gotta get a rise outta you somehow."

We say our goodbyes, then I head to work after Tyler picks up Archer.

As soon as I turn on the lights of the boutique, I post a coupon on my Instagram page. I put in the caption that anyone who shows the image at checkout will receive twenty percent off. Most people are tired of shopping after the holidays, so it's just a little nudge for those who aren't.

By nine, Lexie arrives with a gigantic coffee in her hand. She has sunglasses on, and her posture tells me how hungover she is.

I lift a brow.

"Don't ask," she grumbles.

"Ahh. To be young and twenty-three again. I remember those weekends, but hey, at least you look adorable."

"Is it sad that I told them to add two extra shots of espresso to my latte?"

All I can do is chuckle when she takes off her glasses because she looks rough.

Unfortunately for Lexie, when I open the doors, shoppers flood in.

"I can't believe you posted a coupon! Give a sister a warnin'." She laughs as she rings up a customer. I grab extra inventory from the back while she swipes credit cards. We have a good system and work really well together.

When only a couple of people are browsing in the store, we organize and refold clothes. I'm sure business will pick up again around lunch. It usually does.

"So..." Lexie drawls out. "How's Archer?"

I laugh because she's mentioned him at least once every shift ever since the photo shoot.

"I swear you're like those thirsty cougars on Instagram beggin' me to share his number."

"I love my husband, but if I wasn't married..." She waggles her brows. "Wait, they *really* ask for his number?"

I nod. "Yes! Some drop in my DMs asking for his Snapchat." I don't think Archer even has one.

"They're brave. Well...are you givin' it out or what?" She playfully pulls out her phone.

I scowl at her but laugh. "I mean, the clothes did fly off the shelves, but if it were up to them, they'd be peeling them off Archer's body with their teeth. Damn vultures."

She chuckles with a shrug as she hangs a shirt. "But do you really blame them?"

"Not at all. It's why I respond with the message that he's currently out of stock with no current plans to be available."

Lexie snorts, nearly choking on her own laughter. "You just had a look on your face like he's out of stock for everyone else but you. Don't even lie to me."

I tuck my lips into my mouth, needing to tell someone but knowing that I shouldn't. "Well…" I hesitate for a moment, then decide to just blurt it out. "We've been sleeping with each other."

Her eyes go wide, and she releases a loud gasp. "What! Are you two finally doin' the dirty?"

"Shit, I wish. We're actually sleeping, in the same bed, with no sex."

She gives me a look that says I'm crazy.

"Neither of us likes sleeping alone, and now we're used to it." I shrug like it's not as big of a deal, though every night I get to lie with him is the best night of my life.

"Okay…" Her voice lingers as if she's waiting for more.

"And…" I contemplate telling her the bombshell of the other night. I trust her and have told her things in the past that she'd take to the grave.

She's nearly bursting at the seams. "I won't tell anyone. I swear on my job."

"He kissed me on New Year's Eve," I blurt out.

"Oh my God, how was it?" she asks without taking a breath.

"Everything I ever imagined it'd be. Seriously, he's the *best* kisser." Not to mention how possessive his hands felt on me. "Also, no one else knows except for you, me, and Archer. So, keep your lips sealed, please. I haven't even told Gemma and Katie yet."

"Do you think they'd be against it?"

"I don't think so, but I don't want it getting back to my brother. He's been adamant about Archer getting a fresh start without any outside distractions, aka me." I give her an annoyed look. "I just don't understand why starting over can't include me."

She starts straightening the crumpled jeans on the front table that were picked through this morning. "Well, you know I'm all for it. Plus, I'd rather him be with you than anyone else. He's hot as fuck and so are you. Together, y'all are like one of those Instagram couples. The ones I usually hate too."

"Oh stop," I say with a snort. "I don't know if it's really going to go anywhere. He's determined to stay loyal to my annoying brother."

"But would you want it to?"

I don't even have to think about the answer. "Yes."

"You'd really settle down for Archer?"

I nod with a grin.

"Wow. That's a pretty big deal for you."

"I know, but who in their right mind wouldn't? He's the whole package. Polite, kind, appreciative, protective, sexy as sin." I shrug with a dazed look. "I don't know. There's just something about him and how he makes me feel when we're together. It's not even about what he looks like. It's about how he treats me and makes me feel special. Like I'm the only woman in the world he sees."

"Jesus, woman. You have it bad."

"I know." I stick out my lower lip.

She snickers. "I don't want kids right now, but I'd be happy to let him knock me up."

I continue daydreaming. "Can you imagine how beautiful his babies will be? Whoever he marries will be one lucky lady."

"It could be you, considering you've had his tongue all down your throat," she reminds me.

I groan, grabbing the floor vacuum so I can clean up a little. "Not if Tyler has anything to do with it."

"Did your brother put a lock on your vag? No, he did not," she says assertively. "You can't control what your heart wants. And it sounds like it's mutual if he's kissing you. I don't think you could live with that regret of not trying. No telling what could happen between you two. Marriage and kids. How can Tyler stop you from true happiness?"

"I know," I say, nodding in agreement. She's absolutely right.

Lexie puts her hand on her hip. "He's just being a big brother, and it's none of his business."

"Finally, someone who's willing to take my side." I smirk. "Archer's too afraid to disappoint him. Tyler got him here, his job, and a place to live. He feels like he owes him too much."

"Alright, so you sneak around for a couple of years, then you announce your engagement and pregnancy. What's Tyler gonna do at that point?"

I bark out a laugh. "You're a bad influence, Lex."

I love my brother, and I'd hope at the end of the day, he'd want me to be happy, even if that meant being with his friend. Archer's a grown-ass man and can make his own decisions without Tyler constantly planting seeds of doubt in his mind.

Lexie and I keep chatting as we work. It's nice to have someone I trust to confide in. During that short hour, we restocked the clearance rack with old inventory and tidied the store, though it'll get destroyed again in the next rush. It's been a productive morning, and I haven't been able to stop smiling since our conversation.

Right before noon, the bell above the door rings.

"Good mornin'," Lexie calls out, and I greet the woman with a smile as she looks around.

"We have a buy one, get one pop-up sale on graphic tees if you're a follower on Instagram," I offer with a grin.

"Thanks! I follow you already. Are you Everleigh?"

"I am!" I realize I've never seen her around town before, and I know every person who lives here.

"I found your boutique online and was passing through the area so I thought I'd stop by," she says, as if she read my mind. "I love everything you have. It's so cute!"

"Oh, thank you! Love hearing that."

"Yeah, I was scrolling through your pictures. Do you hire a photographer?" she asks as she browses the racks.

"I actually do them myself."

"You do?" Her eyes light up. "That's pro level! Oh, and that one guy you had on your feed last month. The one with the tattoos…" She lingers, and I see something flash behind her eyes.

I turn and look at Lexie, who smirks with a knowing nod, considering we just had this conversation.

184

"So, what's his name?" she asks, her hand grazing over the graphic tees.

"Archer," I say. "He's never modeled before. Can you believe that?"

"Seriously? He's a natural. Is he...*single*?"

I was waiting for that question.

I chuckle. "Yeah, he is."

"So, he doesn't work here?" she asks as if she was hoping to meet him.

"I don't think he could handle it, honestly," I say with a small laugh. "Just modeled some clothes for me."

She looks around, almost like she's lost.

"Are you looking for anything in particular?" I finally ask.

"Do you have any distressed jeans with rips and stuff?" She wanders over to the jeans that are folded and tucked into cubbies on the wall.

"A girl after my own heart." I lead her over to them.

"You have to try the winter leggings," Lexie interjects. Ever since I gave her that pair, she has literally sold dozens of them.

"Winter leggings?" the woman asks, and I can tell from her accent that she's not from the South. But I can't quite place it either.

"Yeah, they're lined on the inside and keep you toasty warm. I love, love, *love* mine. They're so comfortable," Lexie continues until the woman grabs two pairs.

"I'm sold. Guess I'll take one in black and one in gray." She also grabs a few of the custom sweatshirts that have Ever After Boutique across the chest in a pretty cursive font. I mean, they are cute as hell, but I'm also extremely biased.

After I lead her to the counter and check her out, she speaks up. "I'm Krystal, but my friends call me Kay."

"It's been a pleasure meeting you." I put everything in a

bag. "I also put an extra twenty percent off coupon in there too that doesn't expire until March. I hope you come back."

"Oh wow, thank you so much."

I come from behind the counter and walk to the front. She stays in step with me.

"So, can you tell me anything else about this Archer guy? Does he live here?"

I smile and nod. "Yeah, he does. But he's not really looking for a relationship at the moment."

She sighs. "That's too bad."

"It was nice of you to stop by. Make sure to leave a review online and tag the shop. Would love that!"

"Absolutely. I'm sure you'll see me again sometime soon," Kay says with a hint of something I can't detect.

"I sure hope so!" I offer and give her a wave as she exits.

Lexie comes over to me. "She was so sweet."

"Right! And good upsell with the leggings. I'm totally going to have to give you some more shit to wear," I say.

"Welp, I wouldn't deny the offer."

Lexie's called over by Mrs. Fergurson to see if we have more sizes in the back. I'm pulled away by someone else, and the rush bleeds into our lunch breaks. By the time it calms down again, it's nearly two, and I finally tell Lexie to go eat.

When Lexie returns, it's nearly three, and the shop is empty again. I go in the back and throw a frozen dinner into the microwave and check my Instagram.

My inbox is flooded with questions about Archer once again, and I send them my canned response of the day.

He's currently out of stock, but we still have graphic tees buy one, get one half off.

They usually laugh and don't pester me after that. Today, someone actually came to the shop begging for information, and though she was nice, it came off a little pushy. It's the first time that's happened by a non-local. I hope she didn't come all this way just with the hopes of seeing him.

That'd be creepy.

I can't wait to get home and tell him about it.

CHAPTER SEVENTEEN

ARCHER

"HOW'VE THINGS BEEN GOING?" Annie asks when I call her during my lunch break.

"Great, no complaints." Pretty sure I've never said that before in my life. Though if I'm being honest, things with Everleigh could always improve from friendship to *more*.

"That makes me so happy! So now that you're settled and getting used to civilian life, I'd like to take Everleigh up on that offer and come visit."

I don't think it's a good idea for her to be here since we don't know who's being followed or by who. The last thing I want is for Annie to be caught in the crossfire because of me.

"What if I came to you instead?" I suggest. "I've been wanting to visit Wyoming since you moved."

"Oh, Archer. I'd love that so much and so would Sadie. It's been too long since I've hugged you."

I smile, loving how excited she is. "I'm going to make it happen! Let me see if I can get some time off."

"Yes, please come soon."

"If I can, I will." I promise. Looking at the clock, I realize I need to get ready for my afternoon lesson. My next client will arrive in five minutes.

I tell Annie I'll call her later, and we say our goodbyes. Getting to spend some time with her and Sadie is something I want so badly.

On the way to the boxing room, I stop Tyler.

"Hey, man, I was thinking about planning a trip to go see my sister. Do you think that would be okay?" I ask. "Probably just be a weekend."

"Yeah, of course. Just tell me when and I'll rearrange your schedule. I'm happy you're gonna make some time to see her. I imagine she misses you a lot."

"She does, and I'm looking forward to seeing my niece too. Sadie basically grew up when I was away."

His eyes soften. "I completely understand."

"Thanks, man. I appreciate it."

Tyler gives me a grin before he's pulled away.

As I put on my gloves, Everleigh pops into my thoughts. It's been almost two weeks since I kissed her, and I haven't stopped thinking about how she poured herself into me. It was more than just a friendly kiss, and we both know it. It's hard to forget how I feel when her ass is pressed against me under the blankets every single night, and she moans my name in her sleep.

While I tried to lock her out of my room, the reality is I can't. I love having her sleep next to me. She's become my comfort after a long workday.

Today is exhausting. Since the first, I've shown up earlier and stayed later. By the time I'm finished and clean up my area, it's around seven, and the sun has already set. I walk outside and am completely surprised to see Everleigh waiting in her car for me.

"I could've walked," I tell her when I climb inside.

She playfully rolls her eyes and zooms off. "You're welcome."

"I'm sorry," I say with a laugh. "Thank you. I appreciate it."

She winks. "It was too chilly outside. How was your day?"

"Busy," I say. "Lots of clients."

"Speaking of work—"

"Oh no, you have a look on your face," I interrupt. I'm not able to contain my smile because I have a feeling I know what's coming.

"Soooo, I ordered more clothing for the men's line, and I'd absolutely love it if you could model for me again."

I pop a brow at her. "Do I have a choice?"

"No, not really."

I chuckle, and she playfully shrugs.

"I'd be happy to help, but I'm keeping my clothes on next time."

She parks in the driveway, and we get out. "Hmm. We'll see about that. I swear those abs are what sold the whole stock."

I chuckle because I'll do whatever she needs. I want her to be successful, and if I can contribute in any way after everything she's done for me, I will.

"Just wait until swimsuit season. Speedos are making a comeback," she teases, and I groan.

Once we're inside, I set my duffel bag on the floor and pull out my dirty clothes. Everleigh walks into the kitchen as I go to the laundry room.

When I come back, she's visibly confused and upset.

"You okay?" I ask, getting a glass of water.

"No." She's kneeling beside Sassy who's acting weird. Her

eyes are glazed over, and she's lying around lazily. It's not typical.

"What's goin' on?" I ask, worried about her.

"I think someone was in here. Sassy was chewing on something, and now she's acting all sleepy."

"Why do you think someone was here?" I ask roughly, though I'm trying not to panic.

"Some things in here look like they've been touched. Like the pillow on the couch. The magazines on my table." She lifts Sassy's head in her hands to look into her eyes. "She might need to go to the vet if she keeps acting like this."

"See if she'll drink some water," I suggest, then grab a flashlight. "I'm going to walk around the perimeter to make sure no one's out there."

My adrenaline rushes as soon as I step into the cool air. I pop my knuckles, ready for a fight.

I double-check every window is locked and wasn't tampered with, then I go to the back door, searching for any forced entry points. The backyard and front are clear. Nothing looks out of the ordinary.

I go back inside and check on Sassy.

"Did she eat or drink anything?"

"Yeah, she did. I think she's going to be okay. She's kind of perking up. I'll watch her the rest of the night, and if I need to bring her to the emergency clinic, I will."

I bend down and pet Sassy's head. Her ears lift. "You okay, girl?"

Her nose pushes into my hand.

"Are you hungry? I'll make us something," I tell Everleigh.

She nods. "Starving, but can we just order pizza instead?"

"With pineapple?" I ask with a wink.

"A man after my own heart." She smirks, then places the order. "Did you see anything out of the ordinary outside?"

I shake my head. "Everything looked normal. Nothing broken or forced opened. No footsteps. Is it possible she got her zoomies and was on the couch and coffee table?"

"I don't know, maybe. But I've never seen her act like this. I just have this eerie feeling like someone's been in here. I could've sworn I smelled a perfume that wasn't mine."

I wrinkle my nose, trying to smell what she smells, but I don't notice anything. Since I looked outside, I decide to check around the inside of the house. If anything was moved, I haven't noticed. However, Everleigh knows her house better than I do.

Fifteen minutes later, there's a knock on the door, and Everleigh jumps. Sassy lifts her head, then slowly jumps on the couch. I'm happy to see her moving around.

I take the pizza from the delivery driver and hand him a tip. When I turn around, Everleigh is staring at me with a wide-eyed expression.

"Food and then a shower for you," I order. "You're tense, and you need to try to relax."

"After the Escalade and the detectives and Chad's crazy family, the last thing I can do is relax," she admits. "Maybe I should get a security camera."

"Couldn't hurt," I say.

We sit on the couch and eat slices of greasy pizza with juicy pineapple pieces. It's exactly what we needed. She puts on a show, and we watch in silence. After we're done eating, I put the leftovers in the fridge and meet her back in the living room.

Sassy's lying next to her, still begging for crumbs.

"I think I'm gonna take a shower," I tell her.

"Not a bad idea," she says. "I kinda want to sit in the tub until my skin prunes. Do some meditations or something to calm the hell down before bed."

I grin. "Good. I'll be waiting for you."

After I've showered, I wipe down the kitchen counters while I wait for Everleigh. Exhaustion takes over, so I go lie in bed, fighting sleep until I know she's in here with me.

Finally, she slides under the sheets, and I exhale. Her soft lavender-scented skin presses against mine as I hold her in my arms. Her closeness is calming, and I don't know how I'd adjust if she decided to start sleeping in her room again.

"Feel better?" I mutter.

The moon peeks through the blinds, giving me just enough light to see her gorgeous features. "Yeah, a lot."

I garner up the courage to ask her something that's been on my mind all day.

"I have a question for you…" I linger, swallowing hard.

She studies my face and patiently waits, but I know she's ready to explode inside. That's just how Everleigh is.

"I'd like to go visit Annie and Sadie."

She makes a face, and I find her reaction adorable. "You don't need my permission to see your sister and niece."

I chuckle softly. "Oh, I know that. But I wanted to see if you'd like to join me?"

"Wait, seriously?"

"Well, yeah. She mentioned coming here, but I wasn't sure it was a good idea with everything going on. Plus, it's hard for her to travel with her job and Sadie. Then I thought about leaving you here alone and don't like the idea of that either."

"So, I'm tagging along like a piece of luggage."

I roll my eyes because she likes to mess with me every chance she gets. "Yeah, one big pain in the ass luggage."

KENNEDY FOX

She chuckles. "When would you wanna go?"

"Depends on your schedule. Tyler already told me I could have off whenever."

I watch as she licks her lips and gazes into my eyes.

"What about next weekend? Lexie would cover for me. Dana and Heidi are already scheduled, but they love the extra hours."

"So that's a yes?"

"Absolutely!" Her tone rises with excitement.

"Next weekend is perfect. I already know my sister is going to adore you so much. She's been asking about you ever since we FaceTimed on Christmas."

"I'm going to get her to tell me *all* your secrets." She waggles her brows.

"Never mind, you've officially been uninvited."

Everleigh gives me a look. "Nice try. You're stuck with me."

My smile widens because damn if I don't love the sound of that. "But seriously, thank you. I'm happy you're coming."

I hear Sassy trotting up and down the hallway, pulling my attention away.

"She probably needs to go out again," Everleigh says, moving the covers down to get up.

"I'll take care of it," I offer, standing.

"Alright, hurry back." She pats the bed.

Sassy's tail wags as soon as she sees me and rushes to the back door. She runs into the yard, some of her energy already returning, which is a relief to see.

As I watch her sniff around to find her perfect spot, I smile.

I can't believe Everleigh agreed to come with me to Wyoming. For the past few weeks, I've tried to keep my distance, stay guarded, and not cross any boundaries, but it's becoming impossible.

Taking her with me is nerve-wracking, considering how much I want Annie's approval. I'm not concerned about them not clicking. I'm worried that Annie will like Everleigh *too* much and will give me nonstop grief about not being with her.

When Sassy is finally done, she trots past me back inside. I lock the door and follow her into my room, where Everleigh is waiting.

"I'm glad you're back. Now come snuggle." She lifts the blankets, and I slide right into place.

"Night," I whisper in her ear, and she hums a response.

Leaving Everleigh here alone isn't an option.

I need her just as much as she needs me.

CHAPTER EIGHTEEN

EVERLEIGH

"I'M SO nervous to meet your sister and niece! I hope they like me," I say as we walk into the airport.

"Are you kidding? They're gonna love you. Probably trade me in for you." Archer shoots me a wink. "But seriously, I think Annie and you were separated at birth."

"If that's the case, you and I should stop sharing the same bed." I giggle, but then notice the way his face hardens. "That was a joke, Archer. Relax." I nudge him so he loosens up.

Once we've boarded the plane, I pull out my travel pillow and rest it on his shoulder. "Hope you don't mind me sleeping on your arm."

"No different than any other night." He flashes me a smirk. The weirdness from earlier vaporizes, but the tension still lingers.

Archer rests his head on top of mine after I put in earplugs and get settled. The way he kissed me on New Year's Eve lives in my head rent-free, but that's as far as we can ever let this go. *Even if it's all I think about.*

I feel a tapping on my leg and hear Archer say we're about

to land. Blinking a few times, I look around in disbelief that I slept for three hours. When I lift the window shade, I'm greeted by snowy mountaintops and water. "Wow, how beautiful."

"Annie mentioned taking us on a hike. You'll get some great photos and views of the mountains on the trails."

"You didn't warn me we'd be *hiking* in the freezing cold…" I release a grunt. "But I guess I can try."

Archer chuckles. Though I love staying busy at the shop and being on my feet all day, my adventures are limited to being indoors.

After we land, I schedule an Uber. Archer stays quiet as I take pictures through the back-seat window. He's next to me and so close, I can feel the heat radiate off his body, which feels nice in this chilly weather.

"So, what are you lovely couple going to be doing in Wyoming?" the older man driving asks. "Gonna see the sights?"

"Yeah, a little. Mostly visiting family, though," Archer responds without correcting him.

"Oh, how nice. Make sure you stop by the Tetons. Might be a little bit of a drive, but it's a must-see during this time of year. Could possibly spot some elk."

"That would be great. I've only ever seen the peaks online," I chime in as I continue snapping pictures of snow-covered fields.

The driver drops us off at Annie's apartment complex. Since she's working, she left us a key so we could let ourselves in. "Have you seen her place before?" I ask.

"Nope." He unlocks the door, and we wheel our suitcases inside.

"It's really cute, clean, and smells good. Wow, she should

be an interior decorator," I say, hoping he agrees. I know he wishes he could do more for them, but Annie is used to taking care of herself and Sadie. It's obvious she takes pride in being independent, and I doubt she'd take any help.

"Yeah, but it's also smaller than I imagined." He scratches his cheek as if he's contemplating something.

"No...it's quaint. And cozy," I correct, rolling my bag to the kitchen. "Hope Annie doesn't mind me digging in her fridge."

"Nah, she told us to make ourselves comfortable," Archer reminds me as I grab a drink.

Since she only has two bedrooms, Annie insisted I take Sadie's bed, and Archer's sleeping on the pull-out couch. Sadie will crash with Annie for the two nights we're here. Our arrangements are fine, except I haven't slept alone in weeks.

Archer and I watch TV and doze off some as we wait. Before dinner, Annie and Sadie come home with a couple of pizzas.

"Ah, you're here!" Annie collides with Archer, nearly dropping the food. I take the boxes from her so she can properly hug him.

Archer wraps his arms around her, and I almost choke up because of how happy they look. I understand how hard it can be not to see your sibling.

"Everleigh, so happy to finally meet you in person." Annie grabs me next as Archer lifts Sadie.

"Wow, you grew a foot since I saw you last!" he teases, setting her down.

I follow Annie into the kitchen and put the pizzas on the counter.

"How was the flight?" she asks.

"Great! I slept the whole time." I chuckle. "I love your apartment, by the way."

"Oh, thanks," she says with a small shrug. "It's not much, but it's our home, and it's in one of the better school districts."

"We really need to plan for you to come visit Lawton Ridge," I say. "You'd love it in March or April. There's something magical about the wildflowers that bloom around that time."

"Maybe during Sadie's spring break," she suggests. "I'll have to check if I can get off work first."

"Yeah, we need to go!" Sadie exclaims. "Plus, they have a dog."

I chuckle, kneeling and giving Sadie a hug. "And she would *adore* you."

"Where is she while you're here?" she asks.

"My mimi and pops are dog sitting for the weekend. They've been sending me pics every hour," I tell her with a laugh, then pull out my phone and show her. "See? She's being spoiled rotten."

"She already was," Archer blurts out.

"Of course, Sassy's my little queen." I smirk.

Annie tells us to eat while she changes out of her scrubs. Sadie talks about school and the cute boy she sits next to every day.

"You're too young to like boys," Archer says in a disapproving tone.

"Nuh-uh, Uncle Archer. I'm five. Almost six!" she exclaims. "I'm very *bature* for my age."

I give Archer an amused look as I swallow down my laughter. "A woman who knows what she wants, I love it," I sing-song. "Does he like you back?"

"We're getting married on the playground Monday. I'm going to wear my prettiest dress."

"Excuse me? Are you five or twenty-five?" Archer scowls, and Sadie giggles as she grabs another piece of pizza.

Annie returns in comfy clothes and sighs as she swallows down a bottle of water. "You hear you're gaining a son-in-law?" Archer asks unamused.

"Johnny? Oh yeah. They've been going steady since October." She snickers. "Johnny also has a single daddy who likes to come over for playdates." She waggles her brows, and steam blows from Archer's ears.

"Okay, what? You're both dating, and no one told me?" His voice echoes, and I adore his protective side. It reminds me of Tyler in a way.

"We're *not* dating... We just hang out," Annie insists. "He's still grieving his wife who passed last year, so we're more friends than anything."

Archer points a finger at her, then at Sadie. "No boys."

Annie rolls her eyes, grabs a plate, then meets us at the kitchen table.

"So besides you getting hitched and you being friend-zoned, what else do I need to know?" Archer asks as I open the second box and squeal.

"Pineapple!"

"Archer told me it's your favorite."

"I love you already," I say, taking a slice and inhaling the first bite.

"Don't change the subject. Tell me," Archer insists.

"Nothing, overbearing brother," Annie interjects. "I work, drive Sadie around, do endless loads of laundry, and sleep somewhere between."

"Okay, good," he says, smiling. "Any more sightings of you-know-who?"

"Nope."

I'm lost, so I need to remind him to tell me later.

"Wanna watch a movie?" Sadie asks after we clean up and make our way to the living room.

"Sure, kiddo. What did you have in mind?" Archer pulls her onto his lap as I sit next to them.

"You're gonna regret asking that," Annie muses.

At the same time, Sadie replies, "*Tangled*!"

"Told ya," Annie mutters.

"That's my favorite Disney movie!" I exclaim in all seriousness.

We settle into the couch, and halfway through, Sadie asks for popcorn, so we pause for a break. Once we have snacks and take bathroom breaks, we watch the second half.

By the ending credits, Sadie's passed out in Archer's arms, and I can't deny how my heart flutters when he carries her to Annie's bedroom. Archer is going to be an amazing father. I'm not sure if he wants kids. It's not something we've talked much about.

"Well, I'm exhausted so I'm gonna crash, but you two feel free to stay up as late as you want. Make sure to get some rest because the trails are the best right after sunrise."

"I'll be sure to set my alarm," I taunt, already dreading the elements. "Night, Annie."

Archer returns with a pillow and a blanket. I hate that he's staying on this couch. I'd ask him to join me, but I don't want to sound too attached.

"I'm so tired that I might immediately fall asleep as soon as my head hits the pillow," Archer says, yawning.

"Yeah, same. Gonna wash my face and brush my teeth, then head in too."

Before I can walk away, Archer gently grabs my wrist and

pulls me into his chest. "Thanks again for joining me. Having you here means a lot."

I wrap my arms around his body and feel his heart beating. "Of course. They're amazing. Must run in the family."

"Nah, I don't know about that," he says, pushing away. "But they love you, just like I do."

My breathing stops, and I blink a few times. I know he means that in a friendly way, but that doesn't mean those words don't affect me. Because holy shit, they do.

"Uh, well good night." I swallow hard, then make my way to the bathroom.

After I've brushed my teeth and changed my clothes, I climb into Sadie's bed. Closing my eyes, I count to ten and try to fall asleep, but it doesn't happen. After fifteen minutes of lying here, I grab an extra pillow and wrap my arm around it. Definitely not the same as Archer.

As I'm slowly drifting off, I feel the bed dip, and then the pillow moves out of my hold. When I open one eye, Archer's sliding in next to me. His arm snakes under my body, and he pulls me close.

"What're you doin'?" I whisper, resting my arm over his muscular stomach.

"I didn't want to miss you mumbling my name," he taunts.

"Very funny," I mutter. "I was dreaming about Ashton Kutcher, thank you very much. It just sounded like Archer."

"Oh really?" His chest vibrates with soft laughter. "Ashton from early 2000s or Ashton 2020s?"

I flash a lazy grin. "From *That 70s Show*."

"Oh God, that's bad. He was like twenty when that show premiered. Guess that makes you a cougar."

"He was my teen heartthrob crush," I say with a half-shrug. "Though he's aged like a fine wine."

"Alright, that's enough, maneater. Back to sleep."

"Is that jealousy I hear?" I tease.

Archer wraps his leg over mine, and I instantly relax. "Shush, woman. You need to save your energy for our hiking trip tomorrow."

"Ugh, fine."

His warmth covers me like a blanket, and I instantly drift off.

My eyes snap open as an earthquake rolls through the room. Scratch that, a tiny human who's shaking my shoulder.

"Hi," I say softly.

"Are you awake?" Sadie asks with a bright, hopeful smile.

"Uh, yeah." I blink a few times before sitting up, then quickly look around for Archer. The blankets look like he never snuck in last night.

"Yay! We're about to have breakfast, then go hiking!"

"Can't wait," I grind out between my teeth.

After we eat and get dressed, Annie takes us to one of her favorite trails that's close by.

"When we get to the top, make sure to get out your camera," Annie says. "You'll want to take pics of the view."

"*If* I make it up there, I'm jumping off," I mutter, huffing and out of breath. Between the altitude difference and the cold, I'm dying.

Archer chuckles as he moves in front of me and bends down. "C'mon, hop on."

"What? No, I can't let a five-year-old beat me."

Annie snickers. "To be fair, she has better hiking shoes than you."

I grin. "You have a valid point."

Deciding to take Archer up on his offer, I jump on his back and tightly hang onto him. "Alright, now this is what I call hiking."

Eventually, we make it to the top, and I'm blown away by the view. White powder lightly dusts the surrounding trees, and down below, there's a lake with bluish-green water. Being able to see the mountain peaks in the distance from up here was worth all the work. After we eat a quick snack and drink lots of water, we make our way back down.

"The descent is always easier," Archer says as I pass him on the trail.

At the bottom, we stretch, then get into Annie's car. Once we're back at her place and I take a hot shower, the soreness comes. My calf muscles feel as though they've been twisted and stretched, and it's the first time I've ever used them.

"Doing okay?" Archer asks when I collapse on the couch.

"I-I think so."

Annie sits and meets Archer's eyes. "So, any big plans for your birthday?"

"Wait. When's your birthday?" I nearly jump up. "You didn't say anything about it!"

"Because it's not a big deal." He tries waving me off.

"It's February third," Annie confirms.

My mouth drops open. "That's like two weeks away! Oh my gosh, we need to throw a party!"

"No, I'm good," he deadpans.

"Nice try." I pat his leg. "I'm planning one."

Archer shoots Annie a look, and she glances away innocently.

"Gonna be the *best* birthday ever," I tell him. "You only turn thirty-four once."

He shrugs, then blows out a deep breath. "Don't go crazy."

"Excuse me, have you met me?"

"Yes, and that's why I'm afraid."

I create a new note in my phone. "Archer's Birthday Bonanza," I say aloud as I type. "I assume you'll want to invite all of your gym co-workers. Anyone else?"

"If you're inviting all of them, you gotta invite my cougar clients too," Archer drawls with a cocky grin.

"*Not happenin'*," I snap. "First lesson in business, don't mix it with pleasure."

"She's gotta point," Annie chimes in.

Archer rolls his eyes, and I spend the next hour writing out ideas and making a guest list.

This will be the best party I've ever planned.

The following morning, we eat breakfast together and hang out before we leave for the airport. We could only stay the weekend since we had to get back to work, but it was just what Archer needed. He's missed his sister and niece a lot, and I loved meeting them in person. We've already talked about returning or having them visit Lawton Ridge.

When we board the plane, I put my pillow back on Archer's arm and snuggle in against him. I easily drift off but wake up during some turbulence. Just as I'm about to sit up, I notice he's texting with Annie.

Annie: So, you wanna tell me again how you and Everleigh aren't hooking up?

My eyes widen at her accusation, and I'd be lying if I didn't want to see Archer's response.

Archer: We aren't. I wouldn't lie to you.

Annie: Then do you care to explain why you snuck into her room both nights?

Archer: Were you spying? I was super quiet.

Annie: Ha! Not even gonna deny it. Well, I have super mom hearing. Plus, when I got up to use the bathroom, I noticed your bed was empty. Not hard to put two and two together.

Archer: It's not what it looks like.

Annie: It looks like you two can't stay away from each

other. Just tell Tyler how you feel. I'm sure if you explain everything before he has the chance to hear about it from someone else, he'll respect you a lot more. He'd probably understand too.

Archer: It's more than just Tyler not approving. If we dated and it didn't work out, I'd lose everyone I care about here. I haven't been in a relationship in so long, there's no guarantee I wouldn't fuck it up. Hurting Everleigh is the last thing I want to do.

Annie: Well, if you two are as transparent about your feelings around me as you are around everyone else, I bet he already assumes.

Archer: If he had any inkling of how I felt about his sister, there's not a chance in hell he'd stay quiet about it.

Annie: If you don't try, then you'll never find out if you're perfect for each other. It could crash and burn or you two may live happily ever after. Love is a risk no matter what.

Archer: That's the thing, sis. I do love her. I love her enough not to even chance breaking her heart and ruining her relationship with her family.

My heart is beating so hard, it nearly rips out of my chest. I shouldn't be reading his private messages, but I can't stop now. Not when I've got a peek into his heart.

Annie: I think you're using any excuse to be a coward. You deserve happiness, and you are enough. I know you probably think otherwise because of the past, but I'm being honest. You're the best guy I know.

Archer: You're my sister. Of course you'd think that.

Annie: Everleigh thinks it too. Trust me.

I want to reach into his phone and give Annie the biggest hug right now. It's one thing for me to tell him how amazing he is, but hearing someone else confirm how great we'd be together means this isn't just my imagination.

It's real.

CHAPTER NINETEEN

ARCHER

As EVERLEIGH SLEEPS ON ME, I text Annie, who's determined to drive me crazy. You'd think after spending the weekend with me, she'd get off my back about Everleigh, but I'm afraid it's worse.

Now that she's seen how Everleigh and I are together, she won't drop it. I honestly hadn't realized my attraction was so obvious until now.

"She's right, you know." Everleigh sits up, taking me off guard. "You deserve *everything* you want. You have so much more to offer than you give yourself credit for, and I've fallen so hard for you. Each day, I have to talk myself out of why we can't cross that line, and each day, it gets harder. Listen, I'm scared too, but being together and allowing me to love you could be the best fucking risk we've ever taken."

"Everleigh…" I say quietly, my heart pounding rapidly. I can't believe she read my messages. "We can't do this here."

Being on this plane filled with people is the worst possible place to have this conversation.

She huffs, leaning back into her seat. "She's also right about you being a coward."

I stay silent, clenching my jaw with frustration. Everleigh's the last person I ever want to fight with.

They're both right, though. I *am* being a coward, but I'm also scared of losing her. If I screwed things up, she'd be out of my life forever and so would Tyler.

Once we land in Alabama, neither of us speaks. The walk to her car is full of the same silence. As soon as Everleigh starts the engine, I clear my throat.

"Are you seriously giving me the silent treatment?" I ask.

"No. I just don't have anything to say."

I snort. "I find that extremely hard to believe. You talk my head off most days, and now suddenly you have *nothing* to say?"

She shrugs, pinching her lips together as if she's fighting the urge to tell me off. I don't push her any further as we drive to Lawton Ridge. Before we get home, we stop by her grandparents' house to pick up Sassy. She licks my face, and Everleigh breaks out into a smile. When our eyes meet, she quickly turns and avoids my gaze.

Fuck.

When we get to the house, Everleigh goes to her room. Sassy plops down on the couch, and I unpack. After an hour, I search for Everleigh, but she's still in her room.

"Everleigh," I finally say outside her door. When she doesn't respond, I try the handle, but it's locked. Next, I pound my fist. "Let me in."

She whips open the door, pulling out her AirPods as she scans her eyes up and down the length of my body.

"Jesus. Where's the fire?"

"Well, you weren't answering."

She points at her ears. "I was listenin' to an audiobook. What's up?"

"We need to talk," I say.

"Sorry, I don't think this is the place for that."

I roll my eyes at her attempt to mock what I said earlier. "Don't be like that."

Everleigh crosses her arms, blocking me from entering. "Fine, then what do you want?"

I pinch the bridge of my nose and inhale. "How am I supposed to be with you and hide it from your brother? Or worse, tell him and he kicks my ass, then fires me? What good am I if I'm completely jobless, with no future, and dependent on you?"

She drops her arms, and her eyes soften. "Your job and living arrangements don't make you who you are—your kind heart and genuineness are what make you the Archer I've fallen for. Tyler will get over it. And if he doesn't, find another job. I'm not saying it'd be easy to be together, but don't make excuses because you're scared."

"I *am* fucking scared," I admit. "I'd hate to lose either of you, and you asking me to risk it all puts a ton of pressure on me to make it work. I know how I feel about you and what we could have, but I can't promise I'll be what or who you need."

"I don't wanna have to convince you that it'd be worth trying. Either you want this or you don't." She rests a hand on her hip.

"It's not that easy because all I can think of is what if there's a fallout? What if it ends badly?"

"Okay, and what if it doesn't? Honest question, how will you feel when I meet someone else? You're gonna just sleep across the living room while another man is fucking my brains out? I'm not sure about you, but I couldn't stand seeing you

211

with another woman. That's how I know you're worth the risk. We make it work or we fall apart, but at least we can say we tried."

"Goddammit, Everleigh." I blow out an angered breath, feeling the need to punch something. "Don't put that image in my head because the thought of another man touching you makes me rage." I scrub my hands through my hair, frustration swirling through me. "I have no idea who's following us. It could be someone from my past who's trying to hurt me, which means you could get hurt too. I can't protect you if I'm not thinking straight, and trust me, it's nearly impossible when I'm close to you. I'd never forgive myself if something happened to you because I was careless."

Everleigh closes the gap between us and lifts on her tiptoes, placing a palm on my cheek. Slowly, she presses her lips to mine, and we're glued together for a solid minute.

"Alright, you've made your decision then. I'm not going to beg you. I'd rather you be on the same page, but since you aren't, I won't push further. I'll keep my distance."

She moves past me before I can stop her or respond. I hate that it's come to this, especially after an amazing weekend with my family, but I guess it was inevitable. Eventually, we needed to talk about our feelings and unconventional sleeping arrangement. I just hadn't expected it to be like this.

Later that evening, Everleigh takes a bath, and I get a call from an unknown number. Deciding to answer, I pick it up. "Hello?"

"Is this Archer Boone?" a woman asks.

"Depends who wants to know."

"Are you the man who took away the only important person in my life? My brother."

"Is this Krystal?" I growl, growing angrier.

"You better be on the lookout because I'm coming for who you love, so you'll know exactly how I felt when I lost Chad. You got that, Archer Boone?"

Before I can respond, the call ends.

What the fuck? Now I'm pissed.

I'm undoubtedly convinced she's the one who's been following us. Krystal could've put together how close Everleigh and I are by watching us, but her threats could also be referring to Annie.

How the hell am I supposed to protect my sister from miles away while keeping Everleigh and myself safe?

I contemplate telling Everleigh, but emotions are already so high that I decide against it. She's constantly looking over her shoulder, and the last thing she needs is to be paranoid about a crazy chick who's seeking revenge. Even though she's convinced the SUV is following her, I have a feeling Krystal hired some PI to keep an eye on me. Could've been who was peeping outside of Everleigh's window that night as well. The thought drives me mad.

The only solution I have is telling Tyler the truth about the Escalade and Krystal, and then move. The longer I stay, the more I put Everleigh at risk. If she wants to throw me a birthday party, then I'll wait until after. One last goodbye, then I'll walk away for her sake.

After hours of my thoughts getting the best of me, I call it a night. As I lay in bed, without Everleigh clinging to me, I wonder if I'm capable of leaving. A part of me thinks I should, sooner rather than later, and then another part doesn't want Krystal to win. If she found me here, who's to say she wouldn't if I were somewhere else? I can't live my life in fear.

Just as I'm about to get up and haul Everleigh's stubborn ass in here, my door opens, and she tiptoes inside. I hold back a smirk, knowing that no matter how pissed she is, she'll always come lie with me.

Instead of crawling over me like usual, she stays as far as possible on the opposite side of the mattress. Then she turns and faces the other direction.

Fuck that.

I roll over, slide my arm under her body, and pull our bodies together until we're spooning. When she doesn't fight against me, I brush my other hand over her stomach and find her bare skin. She's wearing one of her skimpy crop tops that she knows I fucking love.

"Don't hate me," I whisper against her ear. "I'm just really trying to do the right thing."

Without replying, she grabs my hand and lowers it over her panties. Of course, she's not wearing bottoms either. I groan, unable to contain my erection.

"Everleigh, don't test me…*please*. I'm begging," I say desperately.

Instead of retreating, she pushes my hand over her wetness. My finger circles over her clit, and she releases a harsh breath. Goddamn, this woman is gonna be my undoing.

"Don't stop, *I'm begging*," she throws my words back.

How can I deny her or say no when this is what we both want? What I've craved for so many weeks?

And how the hell am I going to stop before this gets out of hand?

"This can only happen tonight, you understand?" I say firmly before pulling her earlobe between my teeth.

"I'll agree to anything as long as you touch me, Archer."

Giving Everleigh the pleasure she so desperately wants, I dip my hand inside her panties.

"You're so fucking wet," I growl.

"You do that to me," she admits. "Yes, more of that…"

I rub her eager bud as my own body ignites, but I ignore it. Tonight's about her. If I let her anywhere near my dick, I won't be able to stop her.

"You're so needy," I whisper, then glide down her slit. "You want my fingers inside you?"

"God, yes." She widens her thighs enough to allow me to push two in.

"So tight and wet for me, baby. Goddamn, Everleigh."

"I need more of you," she mutters as she arches her back.

I thrust hard and fast as her orgasm builds. She wraps a hand around my wrist and squeezes it when she's close. Pushing the heel of my palm into her clit, I add more pressure, allowing her to climb closer to her release.

"Let me touch you." She reaches for my cock, but I turn my hips.

"Not a good idea, sweetheart."

"Archer." She moans my name as I add a third digit inside her wet cunt.

"I wanna feel you orgasm on my fingers while screaming my name," I tell her. "This is about *you*."

"I'm close, but I should warn you…" She pants out, spreading her legs more.

"About what?" The words are barely out of my mouth before fluid gushes from her pussy.

"Oh my God," she breathes out harshly, her body shaking.

Holy fuck, she just squirted all over me.

And I loved it.

I continue finger-fucking her until the orgasm dies. She lies on her back, her chest rising and falling. Her whimpers echo between us as I study her.

"That was unexpected," I say with a chuckle. "And so fucking hot."

"Sorry…I tried to warn ya, but…" She shrugs.

"I didn't mind." I bring my fingers to my mouth and lick them clean.

"Your sheets are a mess."

"I'll put them in the wash, and we can sleep in yours tonight," I offer.

"Sounds good. I'm gonna take a quick shower."

Everleigh crawls off the bed, but before she can walk out, I quickly catch up to her and pin her against the door. "I meant what I said," I remind her. "That was a one-time thing."

She sucks in the corner of her lower lip. "You sure about that?"

"Everleigh," I warn. "I'm battling a million demons in my head. Please don't make it harder for me."

She lowers her gaze to my cock that's been hard since she came into my life.

"You can force me away all you want, but in the end, your body *always* gives you away," she says with confidence. And she's not wrong.

I growl out my frustration.

"Feel free to join me in there…we can take turns cleaning each other." She winks, then leaves me with the most tempting offer of my life.

CHAPTER TWENTY

EVERLEIGH

FOR THE PAST TWO WEEKS, I've been in party-planning mode, and tonight's finally the big event. Though his birthday was technically two days ago, we're celebrating this weekend, so we don't have to get up early the next day. I plan to drink my weight in tequila and maybe seduce Archer until we're both naked and sweating.

Against my wishes, Archer has stayed true to his promise he made the night he finger-fucked me. So far, it has only been a one-time thing. That doesn't mean I haven't wished he'd change his mind. One time, he shoved a pillow between us and said if I didn't stop tempting him, it'd stay there permanently. I hated the thought of not being close or touching him, so I promised to behave.

But tonight, all bets are off. Though he doesn't buy into the whole "a year older, a year wiser" mantra, I don't mind being the one to prove him otherwise.

"Birthday boy! Get up, sleepyhead," I call out from the kitchen. I woke up early to make breakfast before the festivities began. I also need to finish decorating before tonight.

"It's not my birthday anymore," he says with a groan, greeting me in only his boxers.

"It's your birthday *month*," I emphasize.

"Oh, man. You're one of *those*." He laughs, reaching for the coffee pot.

"Did you really expect anything else?" I flash him a wink, then hand him a plate of French toast, sausage, and bacon.

"Nope." He happily takes his food and mug. "Thank you. Let me cook for you tomorrow night. I want you to try my meatballs…"

I arch a brow, then lower my gaze down his happy trail that leads me to his…

"…in homemade marinara sauce," he adds with a sly smirk.

"Oh. Damn. But fine. I still owe ya that deli date too. Let's aim for next week so I don't keep forgetting."

"Right. What'd you say I had to try again? Turkey something?" he asks, taking a seat at the table.

"Upside down turkey and gravy sandwich," I confirm, sitting across from him with my food and coffee.

"Sounds good." He licks his finger when he spills syrup on himself. I watch, mesmerized by how his tongue slides along his knuckle, wishing more than anything that he'd use that tongue on me.

"Everything there is, you can't go wrong at the deli," I tell him, then clear my throat. "So, we'll pregame here around seven, then go to the pub around eight, then later, we'll come back for cake."

I've told him the itinerary already, but I repeat it so we're on the same page.

"And why can't I know what kind of cake you made?" he asks around a forkful.

"Because that'd ruin the big reveal!" I smile wide, excited for him to see what I've done.

"You and your parties." He shakes his head with an amused grin.

"Better get used to it. I'm a *go big or go home* kinda gal."

He smirks. "Trust me, I've noticed."

After we finish eating, Archer cleans the kitchen, and I take a shower. My guard is still up, and I keep my blinds closed in case that creepy guy returns. I've seen the SUV twice in the past couple of weeks, but that's it. I don't know if those detectives are following me because I'm a person of interest or if it's someone else.

Archer's been overly protective when we leave the house, which I find adorable and sexy. Keeping my distance has been hard because my feelings for him grow stronger every day. Though he's explained himself several times, I see the way he looks at me. I can feel his walls crumbling—or at least that's what I like to believe.

I curled my hair in beachy waves, my makeup is on fire, and I'm wearing one of my favorite dresses with heels. It took hours to get ready, but Archer's reaction made it worth it.

Right at seven, Gemma and Tyler arrive. Jerry and Belinda are babysitting Scarlett tonight so they can have a good time and celebrate with us.

"Ahhh, you two made it!" I squeal when Noah and Katie arrive.

"By some miracle," Katie says, blowing out a breath as I hug her. "Kinda nervous to be away from the twins for the first time."

"And you're doing great, Mama. Your parents are gonna spoil them and Owen rotten like usual," I reassure her.

Soon, some guys who work at the gym and my employees from the boutique walk in.

"Alright, let's start this party right. Green apple and watermelon shooters." I bring out a tray and carry it around until everyone has one, then I take my own and hold it up. "Happy Birthday, Archer. May this be the greatest year of your life."

Everyone cheers and downs their shots.

Music plays in the background as we drink more and share stories about Archer. He keeps an arm around my waist, keeping me next to him, and even though my brother watches us, he doesn't say anything. When the group gets rowdy, we decide to Uber to the pub. Once we arrive, the party continues.

"If you two are hookin' up, you need to hide it better," Gemma whispers in my ear as we walk to the bathroom. "Tyler's watching you two like a hawk."

"Oh my God. This overprotective big brother act is gettin' old."

Katie stands next to me as I look in the mirror. "Well, are you? Your chemistry is off the charts, babe."

I sigh, contemplating telling them. "We've kissed and fooled around *once*," I admit. "*No sex*."

"Good God, why not?" Lexie blurts out from somewhere behind us. When she exits one of the stalls, I roll my eyes. "Y'all are sharing a bed but not bumping uglies?"

"*What?*" Gemma and Katie shriek at the same time.

"Thanks, Lex," I deadpan, then go back to touching up my makeup.

"We sleep together," I admit. "But like, actually sleep."

"Like…a slumber party?" Katie mocks.

"Yeah, and then we tell each other our deepest, darkest secrets and braid our hair."

They laugh, and I roll my eyes. I shouldn't have said anything, but drunk and horny Everleigh has no filters.

"Honestly, that kinda sounds nice. Just a warm, strong body to snuggle and feel all protected and not so lonely," Gemma says with stars in her eyes. "Tyler and I used to just lie in bed together and talk for hours the first summer we were together. It helped build our foundation."

"As long as you're not left for twelve years," I add with a teasing smirk.

"Yeah, well…" She shrugs. "He came back running and knocked me up, so I can't complain too much."

I snort. "That's one way to look at it."

"All I have to say is you better get out there before Dana claims your man." Lexie gives me a pointed look while washing her hands. "She was getting a little bit too friendly with the arm touching. I think she was asking him about his tats."

"I'd like to see her try, honestly." I shrug, then decide not to take any chances. The rest of the girls follow me out of the bathroom, and I find Dana flirting with Archer at the bar.

"Dana, here's that hemorrhoid cream you were askin' me about. I use it for my under-eye bags, so luckily, I had some with me." I hold it out with a wide smile.

"Um, thanks?" Reluctantly, she grabs it and quickly shoves it into her purse.

"No problem. Hope you feel better soon."

Dana walks away and chats with another table while I sit next to Archer.

"That was some mean girl shit you just pulled," Archer leans in and whispers in amusement.

"Are you saying you wouldn't try to rescue me if the roles were reversed?" I arch a brow, then grab his drink and suck on the straw.

"I've been telling guys at the gym for months now that you're unavailable," he admits, and I nearly choke on his whiskey sour.

"*Excuse me*? They've asked you about me?"

"Yeah, they know I'm rooming with you, so they book a session to get the dirty details about you."

I nudge him with my mouth wide open. "You little vagina blocker!"

"Just protecting you, *roomie*."

I narrow my eyes, wondering what he'd do if a guy really tried to bring me home. "Alright, bet."

He furrows his brows. "What's that mean?"

"You'll see." I pat his shoulder, then walk away to find me a single man.

Sadly, not as easy as it sounds.

A couple of hours later, Tyler and Gemma say good night, followed by Katie and Noah. They're kid-free for the night, so I expect them to fully take advantage of that. Even with them gone, the pub is full, and the party's still going. We're supposed to leave for cake soon, but not until I prove my point to Archer.

"Smith!" I squeal when he walks in with a few friends. "You finally showed up!"

"Yeah, sorry we're so late. Got caught up at a job."

I loop my arm with his, leading him to the bar. "Better late than never. First round's on me."

We take a few shots together, and one of Smith's friends, Cain, offers to buy me a drink.

"Sure, I'll have a rum and Coke."

Archer's on the other side of me, slowly finishing his drink. His eyes burn into me as I give all my attention to Smith and Cain.

"Want a refill?" I turn his way and ask.

"No, I think I'm done after this."

"What? It's not even midnight."

He shrugs. "I don't wanna be hungover tomorrow."

"Well, that's the whole point. It's how you know you had a fantastic birthday."

"So what do you do?" Cain asks me from my other side.

I turn toward him, thanking him for the drink. "I own Ever After. That adorable boutique in the downtown district," I explain.

"Oh, my little sister loves that place."

"Really? You should bring her in some time. I'll hook her up!"

"Yeah? Thanks. She'd love that." He flashes a white smile. "Then maybe we could hang out after? Grab some dinner and drinks?"

Bingo.

Archer's hand finds my waist, and he makes it obvious that he's squeezing my hip.

"I'd love that. Let me give you my number so you can let me know when you're comin'."

Cain hands me his phone, and I input my digits while Archer's jealous eyes peek over my shoulder.

"Cool, thanks." He pockets his phone, then looks around me. "Oh, hey, Archer. Happy Birthday, man."

When I spin around, Archer looks like he wants to stab Cain with his empty beer bottle.

"Hey, Cain. Thanks. Glad you could make it. Didn't bring the wife tonight?"

My heart drops. *Wife?*

"Nah, kept her home with the kids."

Kids?! Oh my God.

"You're married *with* children?" I squeal when I face him.

"Yeah. I heard you liked married men." He flashes me a wink.

"Wow…" I blow out a breath, feeling humiliated and angry. I sleep with one man who ended up being married, and now I'm pegged as a homewrecker. "You better be glad I don't punch your face in and make a scene."

"Archer, control your bitch. *Jesus,*" Cain breathes out.

My eyes widen, and before I can do anything about it, Archer pulls me to the side. His fist twists tightly in Cain's shirt.

"Archer, *don't,*" I say firmly. He can't afford to get into any trouble while on parole. They won't think twice about locking him up again. "He's not worth it."

"No, but you are," he mutters, then drives his fist into Cain's gut.

Cain doubles over, and Smith stands between them. "Cain, leave. Now," he orders, then looks at us. "Archer, *not cool.*"

There's a fire in Archer's eyes, a rage I've never seen before, and it's a little frightening. I only meant to make him jealous, not for him to knock the breath out of the guy.

Without another word, Archer sets a stack of twenties on the bar, then makes his way to the door. I quickly follow, feeling guilty as hell.

"Archer, wait," I plead, rushing in my heels and hoping I don't twist an ankle. "Hold on, I can't run in these."

"What the fuck were you thinking, Everleigh?" he snaps and turns around. His hands are still balled into fists as if he's ready to fight.

"I told you he wasn't worth it! Why'd you punch him?"

"Because he shouldn't get away with calling you names like that," he states. "Cain's a tool, and he had no right to treat you like a piece of meat."

"I can take care of myself, especially when it comes to guys like him. It wouldn't be the first time," I say, wrapping my arms around myself, realizing how cold it is outside.

"Well, you shouldn't have to face it alone. I lost my temper." He steps toward me, closing the space between us. "You drive me fucking crazy. I know you were only trying to get under my skin with that flirty act back there, but the thought of Cain—or *any* man—touching you pushes me into a blind rage. It's something I've tried to hide these past few months because I knew there'd come a time when you'd bring someone home. I've kept trying to convince myself that it was for the best. That any guy who isn't me *would* be better."

I lean against the brick building, trying to control my breathing and warm up. When he notices I'm shivering, he removes his jacket and wraps it around my shoulders.

"Thanks," I say. "And thank you for rescuing me even though I could've handled him on my own."

Archer doesn't move.

His eyes stay glued to mine as his hands cup my face in silence. He looks like he's contemplating if he should lean in or walk away.

To my dismay, he presses his lips to my forehead.

"Let's go home," he mumbles just above a whisper. "You owe me cake."

I let out a small laugh. "Yeah, I guess I do."

CHAPTER TWENTY-ONE

ARCHER

I HAVEN'T LOST my temper like that in months, *years even*, and it only took some asshole eye-fucking Everleigh to make me snap. Cain's one of the gym junkies who comes in almost every day, bragging about how much he can lift and how many phone numbers he gets. Then in the next breath, he'll say what a great dad he is and how his wife gives him midday blow jobs. If I wasn't working, I would've decked him long ago for being a fucking idiot.

After we get back to the house, Everleigh unveils the cake.

"Please don't laugh. I'm still an amateur decorator, but I found this recipe and thought you'd like it," Everleigh says, carrying it to the sofa. She made me close my eyes and promise not to peek.

"I promise I won't laugh," I reassure her. "Can I look now?"

"One second...." she draws out, then clears her throat. "Okay, open."

I lean forward and see it on the coffee table. *"Oh wow..."*

My mouth drops at what I'd undoubtedly call a masterpiece. "What kind is it?"

"It's a triple chocolate layer cake with marshmallow frosting. And there's vanilla marshmallow fluff buttercream between the layers. My first time making it, but I think it turned out okay."

"Just okay?" My jaw is still on the floor. "Everleigh, this looks delicious. I can't believe you did this for me."

"Of course. It's your special day. Well, weekend."

"What's on top?" I ask as Sassy drools next to me. She's ready to devour it in one bite.

"It's things that I thought represented who you are. Boxing gloves, a teddy bear— because you let me snuggle with you every night—" she explains, and we both laugh. "And then a heart, because no matter what, you have mine—whether you take it or not."

I swallow down the huge lump in my throat as I stare up at Everleigh. She's everything I could ever want and more, and here she is, telling me I'm hers.

How can I deny feeling the very same?

"Everleigh…"

"Yes, I know *the rules*. But it's the truth."

I hold out my hand, begging for her to take it. After a moment of hesitation, she finally does, and I pull her to my body until she's straddling my hips.

"Archer," she squeals, nearly sliding off, but I steady her. "I drank my weight in alcohol so—"

Grabbing her face, I brush my lips against hers. I've deprived myself of tasting her for way too long. Even though we kissed on New Year's Eve, it wasn't enough. I wanted —*needed*—more, and I'm sick of holding back.

Everleigh moans as I slip my tongue between her soft lips,

and it makes me feel alive. She rocks against my cock as my other hand slides up her body and cups her breast.

"Fuck, I wanna taste every inch of you."

"Archer, what're you doin'?" she asks as I flatten my tongue along her jawline.

"Kissing you," I answer, then move lower. "Now, I'm sucking your neck."

She chuckles softly. All the blood rushes to my cock as she grinds harder against me.

"Are you sure about this?" she mutters.

I capture her lips, then press my forehead against hers. "I'm so tired of trying to stay away from you, Everleigh. The last thing I want is to wake up one day and see another naked man on the couch because you were sick of waiting for me. Just the thought—or rather, the visual of a man hitting on you —had me losing my mind. I want you as much as you want me, and it's a risk I'm ready to take."

"Not sure if you've noticed, but there's not been another man in my house since the day after we met," she says with a laugh. "I haven't even thought of anyone else since you came into my life. So, if Tyler's the only reason we're holding back, we can deal with him together when the time is right."

I pull back slightly, tucking loose strands of hair behind her ear. "This whole dilemma has put me in a weird spot, but I can't go another day without claiming you as mine. I'll end up going back to prison for taking out every man who dares to look at you."

She bites her bottom lip, rubbing her fingers along the nape of my neck. "As much as I appreciate that, I'd rather keep you in bed, where I need you."

"You just want me for my body heat, is that it?" I flash her a crooked grin, resting my hands on her sides and brushing my fingers under her shirt.

"Well, you know they say, being naked is the best way to get warm."

"So, if anyone asks, it's science."

Her head falls back with laughter, and she nods. "Yes, exactly that."

"Then let's go do an experiment," I suggest, standing and taking her with me. She wraps her legs around me, and I carry her to my room. "We have to get naked, for *science*."

"For science," she agrees as I lay her down on my bed.

I tower over her, eyeing every inch of her gorgeous face. "You really are beautiful, Everleigh. *So goddamn beautiful*."

"So are you, Archer. You have a good heart. I knew that long before I fell for you."

Hearing those words is a flame to my match. "I need inside you, baby."

"God, yes. Been waiting too damn long to hear those words."

I wish I could take it slow, kiss her delicately, and devour every inch. I want to cherish every moment because there may not be more, especially if Tyler finds out. In seconds, Everleigh strips down to her panties, and I tear off my clothes.

"Do you have a condom?" I ask, lazily circling her nipple with my tongue.

"Yes, but I don't want anything between us. I'm on the pill, and I've *always* used protection."

Lord, she's going to kill me. I should ask for forgiveness now, but I'd gladly go to hell for her.

"You're sure?" I ask.

"Yes, Archer. You're more than just a hookup for me."

I lean up on my elbows and gaze into her lust-filled blue eyes. "That's the last fucking thing you'd ever be for me."

"I know. I trust you."

Her words send a wave of warmth through my body. No one I've dated has ever put so much faith in me before.

Unable to fully express how much her words mean to me, I lower down her body, kissing a trail to her pussy. I spread her thighs and press my lips against the thin fabric.

"You gonna squirt for me, sweetheart?"

"Mm…put your mouth on me and find out," she taunts.

With my tongue, I tease her needy clit over her panties. She wiggles and arches her back, seeking relief, but I'm not ready to give it to her yet. Everleigh grabs my head, keeping my mouth right where she wants it.

"Archer, I swear to God, if you don't—"

Before she can finish that demanding sentence, I twist my fingers on each side of her panties and rip off the thin cotton.

"Did you just…?"

"You were threatening me, so I had to act fast," I respond innocently.

"Fuck it, I don't care." She widens her legs. "More."

"*Tsk. Tsk.* What's the magic word?" I blow over her sensitive clit.

"Goddamn you," she hisses, lowering her hand down, but I swat it away. "Now?"

I brush the pad of my finger over her bud, then down her slit but don't push inside. "Gotta do better than that, baby," I say, sliding my tongue through her wetness.

"Fuck me, please. Please. Oh my God, *please*!"

"That's my good girl. I like it when you beg. Now for your reward," I muse, driving two fingers deep into her cunt.

"Ah," she gasps as her body nearly flies off the bed. She fists the sheets as she rides my hand. "Yes, right there."

Now that I'm fully prepared for her to squirt all over me, I can't wait.

As I finger-fuck her, I suck on her throbbing clit, swirling my tongue around and tasting every inch of her pussy. Everleigh's responsive as hell, and my dick is so rock hard that it might break going inside her.

"My greedy little girl. You wanna fuck my face? I want your come all over me."

"Holy shit, *yes*…" She pants, her chest rising and falling as she struggles to catch her breath. "So close, oh God."

Before I can continue praising her, Everleigh's thighs tighten around my head, and she stills. Seconds later, she's spilling out and screaming out her release.

I don't care that part of the bed is wet. Standing, I reposition her until she's bent over the other side of the mattress. "Jesus Christ, that was sexy," I murmur in her ear as my hand rubs between her thighs. "Spread wide, baby."

She does as she's told, and I give her ass a good slap. It immediately turns red, and I slap the other. I grip my shaft and stroke it a few times before pushing the tip against her entrance. Momentarily, I stall and suck in a deep breath before coating myself in her come.

"Ready?"

She responds by grinding back against me and lowering herself onto me. "Fuck, Everleigh." I groan out. "Your cunt is so wet."

I push in deeper, feeling the softness of her skin and the way she tightens around me.

"Shit," she moans. "Deeper."

With a hand on her hip, I impale my cock all the way inside

her. She nearly collapses on the bed with a grunt but holds herself up as I thrust faster.

"Is this what you wanted, baby?" I press down on her lower back to keep her steady. My other hand rubs her clit as I thrust harder.

"Yes, so much yes."

Everleigh moves against me, and our bodies smack together as our moans echo. I flatten my chest over her back as I capture her mouth, the taste of our sweat intermixing. Her muscles flex while her breaths grow more ragged.

"Yes, baby. Come on my cock," I encourage as I bite on her lower lip. "You're so ready."

Within seconds, she does. Her convulsions nearly rip me in half as I focus not to release inside her yet.

Once her breathing steadies, I bring us to our feet and kiss her senseless. "I've wanted to fuck you against that wall for weeks now." I lift her, and her legs wrap around me. I press her back against the part of the room that doesn't have any pictures hanging.

"Please do," she begs. "I plan to have you on every inch of this house."

"Sounds like a goddamn plan to me."

I thrust back inside her, sucking her neck and chest as we rock together. My feelings for Everleigh grew so damn fast and are so strong, I can't imagine ever giving her up now. Especially after being inside her, having her squirt around me, and knowing what she tastes like. We're risking everything, but this—her—is a risk worth taking.

"Everleigh," I whisper as we pant for air.

"Hmm?" Her arms stay wrapped tightly around me.

"Aside from protecting my sister, falling for you is one thing I'll never regret in life. No matter what happens."

She stares at me as if she's waiting for a bomb to detonate. I don't blame her. After holding back all this time, now I'm putting it all out there.

"So deeply, irresponsibly in love with you," I continue.

Our mouths crash together and fuse as one as I taste her sweetness and fuck her senseless. The way she makes me feel is like nothing I've ever felt before.

"I'm in love with you too, Archer. Have been for a while," she says when we come up for air.

"Fuck, those words are gonna have me—" I hiss through my teeth as the most intense orgasm takes over. My body stills as I fill her deeply, her nails digging into my shoulder blades. Soon, she's jumping off the edge with me.

Everleigh's legs go limp as we fight for oxygen, and my arms numbly bring her feet to the floor. "Wow," I pant, cupping her cheeks and bringing her mouth to mine for a quick kiss.

"I can't believe that just happened…" she admits.

Before I can say another word, a loud crash comes from the living room.

What the hell?

"What was that?" she whispers in a panic.

"Stay here. Let me go check it out first." I quickly pull my boxers on.

Opening the door, I poke my head out, then tiptoe to the living room. There I find the criminal.

"Oh shit, you're in trouble now," I say, trying to hold back my laughter. Sassy's knocked over the birthday cake and is inhaling it by the mouthful.

"Well?" Everleigh whispers.

"It's just Sassy," I tell her.

Everleigh comes out and gasps. "No! Bad girl!" She tries to push Sassy away, but the hungry little shit is insistent.

Deciding to get involved, I grab Sassy's collar and yank her away from the chocolate feast.

"You're not supposed to have that!" Everleigh scolds. "Now I have to watch her and make sure she doesn't get sick."

Once I've taken Sassy out, I return to a pouting Everleigh staring at the messy floor. "That was supposed to be *your* cake."

I wrap my arms around her waist from behind, then kiss the nape of her neck. "You know what would be fun? Taking whatever she hasn't slobbered on and eating it off your body. Then after, we can share a shower."

"Archer Boone..." she sing-songs, spinning around and locking her fingers behind my head. "Have I awoken the beast?"

I release a deep growl, leaning in to capture her lips. "You most certainly have."

After a never-ending perfect night of eating chocolate off Everleigh's sexy curves and then washing off every inch of her in the bath, we collapse in her bed, sated and exhausted. I lost count of how many rounds we went last night, but it never felt like enough. I wanted more, she teased and seduced me, and I pleased her multiple times over.

Now that I've had her, I'm not letting her go. I only hope Tyler will understand.

"Morning," I say softly when she rustles next to me.

"Good mornin', handsome," she coos, her hand sliding down to the erection waiting for her. "I'm addicted to this now."

"I think it's addicted to *you*." I groan when she wraps her hand around my shaft, sliding up and down, then focuses on the tip. Fuck, I'm so sensitive to her touch.

"Guess there's no hope for us then. No amount of rehab can cure it," she says.

I roll until I'm towering over her. "I'm good with that. How about you?"

"I sure am…as long as—"

The doorbell ringing along with Sassy barking interrupts us.

"Oh, that must be the breakfast I ordered. I scheduled it yesterday, pre-sexathon, but thank God I did. My body is way too sore to cook today."

"Why'd you do that?" I ask as she quickly puts on her robe.

"Well, I figured we were gonna get super drunk last night and would need post-birthday activities food to soak up the booze."

Chuckling, I stand and reach for my boxers. "Good call. I'm gonna use the bathroom, then I'll meet you in the kitchen." I press my lips to hers before I go.

Everleigh greets Sassy on the couch, then makes her way to the front door. Her voice goes up an octave, and it takes me a minute to realize she's not talking to a delivery person.

"What do you have that I don't have?" a woman's voice asks.

"What are *you* doing here?" Everleigh asks.

Deciding to skip the bathroom, I walk toward her, wanting to find out what's going on.

"What do you have that I don't have!" the woman repeats, but now she's screaming.

"Is there a prob—" I move behind Everleigh, widening the door, just as my eyes land on a woman who looks cracked the fuck out. She takes a step forward. Before I can comprehend what's happening, Everleigh inhales a harsh breath, then slowly crumples to the floor.

"Baby," I rush out, trying to catch her.

The woman runs off, and I look up to see the black SUV speeding away.

When I glance down at Everleigh, she's holding her stomach, and that's when I notice the pool of blood around her fingers.

"What…what happened?" My eyes scan over her quickly as I peel back the fabric of her robe. "Baby, what'd she…" And then I see it. "She fucking stabbed you!"

Everleigh's eyes close, and I shake her shoulders. "No, stay awake. I gotta get my phone. Stay with me."

She's losing too much blood too fast.

I rush toward my cell, then dial 911.

"Everleigh, look at me." Her eyes flutter open, then shut. "Everleigh." I put my hands over the wound and apply pressure, but the bleeding continues.

"911, what's your emergency?" the dispatcher answers, but my attention is glued to Everleigh.

"I-I love you," she mutters.

"Don't you dare," I grind out. "You stay with me."

"Hello, what's the location of your emergency?" The dispatcher speaks louder, but my heart is ripping to shreds, and I can't focus.

"I love you, Archer."

And then she loses consciousness.

———

Continue Archer & Everleigh's story in *Wanting You Close*

If you haven't started from the beginning, you can read Tyler & Gemma's and Noah & Katie's duets now.

AVAILABLE NOW

**Continue Archer & Everleigh's story
in *Wanting You Close***

I never imagined my new roommate would be the man I'd actually fall for. Though I don't get close to the people I sleep with, he's been my exception. Archer acts emotionally unavailable while he focuses on starting over, but our connection is too strong to ignore.

He's rugged on the outside and sweet on the inside—the opposite of my usual type. I see the way his eyes gaze up and down my body, making it harder to keep my feelings in check. Knocking down his walls is no easy task, especially with my brother interfering, but I refuse to give up.

When lines are crossed and emotions bubble over, trouble finds us. We both have pasts that have leaked into our present —now I'm scared it'll destroy the one secret we've been keeping.

ABOUT THE AUTHOR

Brooke Cumberland and Lyra Parish are a duo of romance authors under the *USA Today* pseudonym, Kennedy Fox. Their characters will make you blush and your heart melt. Cowboys in tight jeans are their kryptonite. They always guarantee a happily ever after!

CONNECT WITH US

Find us on our website:
kennedyfoxbooks.com

Subscribe to our newsletter:
kennedyfoxbooks.com/newsletter

[f] facebook.com/kennedyfoxbooks

[twitter] twitter.com/kennedyfoxbooks

[instagram] instagram.com/kennedyfoxduo

[a] amazon.com/author/kennedyfoxbooks

[g] goodreads.com/kennedyfox

[BB] bookbub.com/authors/kennedy-fox

BOOKS BY KENNEDY FOX

DUET SERIES (BEST READ IN ORDER)

CHECKMATE DUET SERIES

ROOMMATE DUET SERIES

LAWTON RIDGE DUET SERIES

INTERCONNECTED STAND-ALONES

BISHOP BROTHERS SERIES

CIRCLE B RANCH SERIES

BISHOP FAMILY ORIGIN

LOVE IN ISOLATION SERIES

ONLY ONE SERIES

MAKE ME SERIES

Find the entire Kennedy Fox reading order at
Kennedyfoxbooks.com/reading-order